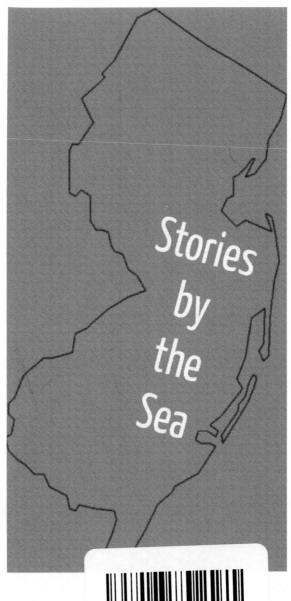

Stories
by
the
Sea

eNJoy

Stories by the Sea

Glen Binger

Bing Bang Books © 2017
@bingbangbooks

1st edition: June 2017

Bing Bang Co.
New Jersey

Glen Binger
glenbinger.blogspot.com
@glenbinger

Also by Glen Binger

Figment

Only Human: Stories of Weakness

The Definition of Me

Attributes Statement

This is a work of fiction. These stories use names and places as public knowledge to illustrate a sense of relatability specific to New Jersey. No malice or defamation is intended towards any of the public figures or establishments mentioned. In no way, shape, or form were they meant to disrespect, libel, or slander the latter parties. The situations in which they appear are completely fictional. The collection is imaginary narrative from the author's own anomalous mind. Any resemblance to actual events is entirely coincidental and unintended in every way. **eNJoy.**

All Rights Reserved

Praise for *eNJoy: Stories by the Sea*

"Author Glen Binger is the quintessential 'Jersey Boy.' These writings - these first-hand, whimsy accounts of the Jersey Shore - are a proverbial breath of (salty) fresh air. The jetty comes alive, the gulls squawk, the mysterious waves calm the soul in this collection. *eNJoy* isn't just a book for the summer reader, it's for the true New Jersian year 'round. I cannot wait for what Binger has in store for me in the near future."

> ➢ Joseph A. Federico, Founder & president of *Anchors To Dusk Publishing*, author of *Voudou Juice*, co-author of *Images of America: Galloway Township* by Arcadia Publishing.

"Glen Binger is so desperate he wrote a book. Well, *I'll* read it. It's a collection of short stories, after all. If there's water at the shore, Glen Binger will find it, sure as he's out there pointing his metal detector toward character, plot, and prose. I'm a semiliterate alcoholic, a realistically stupid man of letters. But, goddammit, Glen Binger is so good he can write his way off a dirt road and onto a New York City taco truck. Shit."

> ➢ Mickey Hess, author of *The Nostalgia Echo* and *The Dirty Version: On Stage, in the Studio, and in the Streets with Ol' Dirty Bastard*.

"Binger's writing is an old friend. The friend who reminds you that it was cool to like New Found Glory at one point in your life and it's OK that you also like Cable TV now that you're older."

> ➢ Leonard Walker, writer

"I love the beach. I love (the idea of) Jersey. Glen brings the overlooked nuances of both to this book."

> Josh Spilker, author of *Taco Jehovah*

"Having read Glen Binger's new collection *eNJoy* I now believe that we can only achieve true happiness when our feet are dangling in the ocean and we have an ice coffee in hand. I also believe that everything one needs to know about girls, pork rolls and the meaning of life can be found on the beaches of the Jersey shore."

> Ben Tanzer, author of *Be Cool - a memoir (sort of)* and *SEX AND DEATH*

Acknowledgements and Thank Yous

There are entirely too many people to thank. So many awesome human beings, with or without their knowledge, have helped me create this book. I cannot even begin to list all of them. Rather, I'd like to thank everyone who has taken the moment to share a human moment with me. Anyone who has unleashed their mindfulness, their honesty, and/or their sincerity. Whether that's in deep conversation or by simply picking up this book. I truly appreciate you and all that you've done to help me grow as a human being. Much love.

Special shoutout to those who specifically aided the creation of this book: Ben Tanzer, Mickey Hess, Joe Federico, Josh Spilker, Leonard Walker, Tom Adams, Peter Erich, Eric Keegan, Carl Bivona, Allison Ripoll.

+++ **good vibes only** +++

For B --- bringing me closer to the edge. *I'd be lost without you next to me by the sea.*

Table of Contents

Introduction

Let me first acknowledge that this collection will not be for everyone. It is not your typical beach read, even though most of it was written on the beach. It isn't the same literary lexicon you might find on a Top 10 shelf next to Ray Bradbury or J.K. Rowling.

To be honest, I can't quite tell you what it is. I just don't know.

… It simply is.

The real reason this book exists is because you do. You were born. You learned how to read. You found it by some means of fate. And then you decided to lend me a small portion of attention. For that, I am truly grateful and thank you from the bottom of my heart.

Talk about niche audience, though. I mean shit. These are stories from Jersey. More specifically, ones about living near the ocean and all the density that comes with it. It's where words and worlds become clear for me. Where I was born and bred and where I feel most at home. It is where I'll likely die too. Here by the sea, my mind can either run wild or float wanderly, depending on the tide.

These stories are my vessels. Some of them are rooted in truth. Some of them are entirely fiction.

Others aren't really anything. They peacefully exist, waiting for you to figure that all out.

I know, I know. I know what you're thinking. No one reads short stories anymore. Nobody cares where they came from or what they're about. *Blah, blah, blah.* Please realize that isn't exactly what I'm going for here. This was not created for "the industry." I wrote this because I needed to. Because the ocean is in my blood and it needed canvas to spill upon.

It keeps me buoyant.

Rather, these are small pieces of human condition, scattered in the sand with shells and sea glass at dusk. They're chunks of energy born out of sunsets and mindfulness.

It started with an epiphany "On Ocean Ave" and ended sometime during the "Reflections of Summer." I couldn't stop writing if I wanted to. The project began as an attempt to convey something - a feeling, an emotion, a love-affair - one that I'd never been able to effectively and efficiently explain to anyone. Even to the ones who claim to "get it." *In fact*, the only people who ever seem to understand are the ones who live in or come from such coastal habitats. And sometimes they can't find the right words either. So I figured I'd try.

I remember being a freshman in college at Rider University, out by Princeton, trying to explain this to friends from Philly or New York. It would go like this:

> "So where are you from?"
>
> "Manasquan, by the beach."
>
> "No, not your summer house. Like real home."
>
> "Yeah. That's where."
>
> "Wait… people live there all year round?"
>
> "Yep. We have dentists too."

And then I'd shake my head, upset with the world, wondering why I even bother.

I feel like some (all) of the major media outlets like Bravo, MTV, and HBO gave us a bad rep. (On top of all the other previously established and well-deserved ridicule.) They portrayed a culture that only exists in a small percentage of New Jersey, only adding more fuel to the jokes. The term "jersey shore" used have a positive connotation. Now, unfortunately the rest of the country - and perhaps world - think we're all fist-pumping wannabe Italians who enjoy tanning, excessive wealth, and beating women. Or we're just America's armpit and serve no purpose. All they know is the Turnpike, Parkway, and putrid smells in between. Or that **big** governor guy, Chris Christie, who gave up campaigning for president to endorse Trump.

While some of these stereotypes definitely exist here throughout certain seasons (namely May-August), it does not identify with what cultures truly stem from the Jersey Shore. Especially after Hurricane Sandy. It's just its own thing.

So then what does true Jersey stand for? Springsteen and Sinatra? The Parkway? Pork roll, egg, and cheese?

I sure as hell have no idea. I can't explain what it's like to be here. I can't describe anyone else's thoughts besides my own. But I can tell you one thing: if you ask anyone from the Jersey Shore why they live here (and haven't left yet), they can't quite put their finger on it. Maybe they'll have a few Jersey-pride stories. Or some weird-accent NSFW vernacular. Maybe they'll talk about the beach lifestyle or the surf. I know my dad has more lifeguard stories than my mom cares for. Some might even tell you about all the farms we used to have. Others might explain what it's like to have someone else pump your gas. No matter the response, one truth is simple: living here is like anywhere else. (Except it's really not.)

***

I've been experimenting with different podcasts on my commute lately, and I stumbled upon the infamous Joe Rogan Experience. Joe Rogan is a TV personality and comedian, known for his work with *Fear Factor* and UFC Commentary. In my recommended cache, I found an episode that he did with Tim Ferriss, author of *The 4-Hour Workweek*. About 20 minutes in, Rogan is talking to

Ferriss about creating home-disaster kits, just bullshitting as Rogan typically does on his podcast, talking about life being fragile and totally random. Ferriss brings up Hurricane Sandy's recent destruction at time of the podcast release (November 18, 2012) and, of course, my ears rang. What I heard is something that might help to explain the concept of this book you are holding. Here it is:

(I translated from Rogan's super-stoned, verbal gibberish just to make it readable; but the gist is there.)

"I have a friend who has a vacation house on the beach in Malibu. It's so badass. You sit there and you're like **on** the ocean. And it's such a humbling experience; it's like something that connects you in some weird way to nature when you're staring at that water. I think that's why beach communities are so chill. Beach communities are everyday confronted with this reality that you aren't shit. You stop and look out there as far as you can see **is water**. And you **die** out there. You can't make it. And, if for some reason, it just swishes back and forth a little it's gonna wipe out everything for 100 miles in **like it's nothing**. Ok? So settle the fuck down. And ***stop taking yourself so seriously***. Like that's the feeling that you get when you're right next to water. I think that's important for people. I don't know. It gives you a feeling. A real peaceful feeling."

***

In any case, welcome, friend, dear reader. The fact that you're even here means more than you can ever imagine. Thank you for reading at least those 1000 words.

This collection was curated with several purposes and concepts in mind. Again, none of which I will ever be able explain to you. Art is meant to be interpreted. According to Google, it's defined as: "...the expression or application of human creative skill and imagination, typically in a visual form such as painting or sculpture, producing works to be appreciated primarily for their beauty or emotional power." While I might never possess such power, the interpretation of what you are about to read is on you. I can't tell you how to do that. I'm only trying to help you think.

Rather, what I can tell you, is that this book is a mere snippet of human condition at the Jersey Shore. A little slice of life from some guy with a funny last name. Writing about it is all I know how to do. And sometimes I don't think that does it enough justice. Henceforth, I will cease referring to it as "the shore." Where I'm from, it's known as "the beach." In fact, I've probably already lost credibility amongst my locals for saying it so many times. Sorry friends.

16

In actuality, this book is for *you*. It bleeds sand and salt water, with an overpopulated understanding of what it is *truly* like to live here on the east coast edge of America. We all know what MTV did to further ruin the reputation of the Garden State. Not that anyone thought it could be worse than the smelly armpit without purpose. But here we are.

If I've learned anything from composing this collection, it is this: be present and eNJoy whatever you're doing and whoever you're doing it with. In the end that's all we have. Mindfulness is a skill like anything else. You can get better at it.

Although this book is dedicated to those who already know what it's like to live here, to grow up here, and to possibly die here - it isn't *for* them. It's for anyone who gives a damn. For the people whose attention span lasts longer than 140 characters and/or 15 seconds of commercial time. For the people with a head on their goddamn shoulders. You don't need to *live here* in order to read this. You don't *need* to be a *local*. You don't need to *pretend to be* either. The only thing I'd recommend is to have an *open mind*. And perhaps an appreciation for the arts of literacy. New Jersey is my vehicle - my lens - in which I attempt to assimilate some sense of the universe around me. (Maybe some nonsense too.) This book will not explain what it's like to live here, oceanside and salty. For that, you'll have to ask someone who can put it into words. Because I sure as hell can't.

All I ask is that you **eNJoy**…

On Ocean Ave

I took the long way home so I could cruise south along Ocean Ave and hear the shorebreak. I just needed it, you know?

It was a sparse April sunset, peeling warm at the right side of my face. My Jeep was brand new at the time; only had 2500 miles on it, not even rusted over by the air yet. You'd better believe I made sure the windows were down.

Hell, I almost took the top off.

There was something about it. The air, the water - that salty smell that always knew how to put you in the right state of mind. Whether high tide or low, it could wrap your heart in tin-foil vitality if you wanted. If you let it in.

Not everybody "gets it." Even some of the other locals. It's never easy to explain. And, to be honest, I suppose it's different for everyone.

Could be the way light refracts between whitecaps. Or maybe the cadenced patterns of the waves polishing more pebbles. My fiancee claims it's how the water whooshes away after melting her toes. For me, it's that feeling my lungs get after inhaling the deep, endless horizon.

My Jeep liked her top down. But it was too soon for that. (I knew better.)

April was coming to a close. Eventually it'd be May; which meant riding bikes. And drinking cold beers in warm sunshine. I couldn't wait. Every year, right around this time, my patience is always put to some sort of [insignificant] universal test. I think I passed this year.

It was just another Wednesday. A tiresome sack of time where finding my breath felt like a chore. I was exhausted from teaching, coaching, and editing an article for the local beach blog. And, on top of all that, I had to catch an interview appointment before I could head home for dinner. It of course ran a little longer than planned.

"Hey babe can you stop for milk?" Allison texted me.

The bluetooth was programmed to read messages aloud, but always pronounced "Allison" as "Allie-sun." Made me laugh even though I wasn't in a great mood.

"All hail Allie-sun," I said, gesturing like a robot to no one.

I pulled over (facing the ocean of course) and typed out "why can't you" with extra sass by leaving off the punctuation. Why? I don't know - it wasn't even something inconvenient. I'd be passing two 7-11s, a QuickChek, and the local Sunrise Mart on my way home. Somehow I'd psychologically evolved into a dick when I was tired. *Thanks genepool.* If I was 17 again, I'd probably have sent it too, not knowing any better.

But I didn't. I'd grown as a person throughout my late 20's. I was used to the hustle. The grit. The ocean changed me in ways I'd never be able to explain.

Instead I took a deep breath, inhaling the sea and the earth and every atom of matter in between, and responded simply; "Sure babe, no prob. See you in a bit"

"Thanks," she wrote back. "Love you to the beach and back!"

Allison might never be aware of this epiphany (at least until she reads this). It isn't easy to admit. In fact, it's kind of embarrassing. Makes you feel vulnerable. Like nothing in the world can cure you. But I guess that is part of being human: to recognize when you're being an asshole and adjust yourself accordingly. Clearly not everyone has the latter part figured out.

I took one more deep breath and backed out onto Ocean Ave. It was lowtide so I drove slower, with a big dumb smile on my face.

Sunrise Mart was quiet. I reflected on my sudden mindfulness staring at the cold box. It was a soft skill I'd only developed after college. A line drawn in the sand between my ego and my empathy.

Patience dude. Come on. She only let you know we needed milk. No crisis here. Besides having nothing to put in tomorrow morning's coffee. No stress, no stress. Be easy. Man the Sunrise milk game is on point. Did I leave the car unlocked? How much cash do I have? I wonder what time low tide this weekend...

I can't allocate this mindset to living by the beach. I can't say it's because I have sea in my soul. You wouldn't believe me. I have no concrete evidence. But I can tell you that living oceanside helps me to realize that in itself. Just like it always has.

Countless times I'd succumbed to late night beach walks out of depression or sadness. (Out of happiness too.) It's daunting to gaze out into a darkness so massive that stars graze the horizon like pebbles. Makes you see yourself for what you really are. Reminds you of your human.

One of my favorite authors, Mr. Jack Kerouac, once wrote, "No human words bespeak / the token sorrow older / than old this wave / becrashing smarts the / sand with plosh of twirléd sandy / thought," (poem: "Sea" from 1962's *Big Sur*).

That night, I found my human. I drove home and kissed Allison and stuck the milk in the fridge, remembering that "man suffers only because he takes seriously what the gods made for fun," as Alan Watts has expressed, probably after one of *his* tests.

I passed mine. There grew something in my heart that I might never be able to get out. The sun and the moon, a memory of stars opaque with blue, soaking my heart like white blood cells.

Maybe you feel this too. Maybe you don't. It's okay. I know one thing is true: that feeling I get with the salty air in my lungs - it will forever massage the molecules of my spiritual identity. Every fucking time. I can only hope you too might one day experience something so malleable.

At the very least, roll your windows down when you're on Ocean Ave and try. Just don't forget the milk.

By Sundown

As the sun pillowed treetops across the river, that sinking feeling of bedtime crept up my guts. "We have to go," said my little brother Emmett. "Mom said by sundown."

From the time I was old enough to leave the yard, but not the neighborhood, I found escapable solace in a place where all the block kids of that age went: a boat launching dock and small park just on the other side of the grid. Kids went there with ambitions of being unsupervised. It is where many of us learned our first curse word or had our first kiss, back behind the swing set. It was a time without household internet access.

I remember trying to catch lightning bugs back there with my younger brother one night - the absolute best spot in the whoooole neighborhood for 'em too. Probably because it was so close to the water. You could smell the ocean just a few blocks east.

"Relax, it'll be fine," I told him.

I knew we'd be grounded. Deep down inside, at 12, I had yet to develop my sense of empathy.

"But what if mom grounds us?"

"Relax," I lied again. "It'll be fun."

I only wanted to stay because I had a crush on the girl who lived two blocks over on Maple St. Anna. She was there with her brother, catching lightning bugs in mason jars like us.

"Alright if you say so."

Eventually the sun slipped apart and sunk behind tree trunks and houses, dimming everything as the lightning bugs nestled back into grass. Anna and her brother went off smiling, not worried about being grounded or getting in trouble. We'd see them again... one day. Emmett and I left for what might've been the longest walk of my 12th year on planet Earth.

As expected, our mother stood at the door, waiting to tug on our ears with the force of a thousand suns, armed with the words "You're Grounded" at her lips, ready to fire.

Emmett, upon being released of Apollo's grip, immediately burst into tears and ran to his room. I tried to escape but still burned at the flesh of my ear.

"Christopher James," she said - the middle name always an added threat. "You know better than this. Far beyond being pissed off!" She guilted, that disappointed glare in her eyes, "Your brother is too young to learn such defiance. Look what have you taught him!"

I was speechless - from fear and physical agony - but from this sudden awakening too. The influence on my brother's young mind. I'd never realized.

"I *know* that this was not his doing," she continued, finally letting go. "You best march your butt upstairs and apologize. If you're lucky, he'll continue to admire you the way he always has."

They say a mother always knows.

Upstairs, I knocked on Emmett's door, something I'd never done. "Go away!" he yelled.

"Emmett, let me in."

"I said GO AWAY!"

"Emmett, I'm sorry."

No words, only sniffles.

"I'm sorry, Em. Really."

More sniffles.

"I'll make it up to you."

Less sniffles, still silent. I left him alone, hoping he'd eventually forgive me. The sunset would soon paint our faces again, and *again* provide new opportunity to demonstrate self-discovered empathy. The world spins away; my actions still more than simple actions.

That following week, later in July, after being freed from the house, we caught more fireflies down by the river. Anna was there again too. But this time, when the sun dropped below the treetops, I turned to Emmett; "Hey, let's go before mom gets mad again."

He said, "No let's stay." As if he'd totally forgotten what happened the previous weekend.

"Nah, I don't want to be grounded for another week."

"Oh yeah! Me either, that sucked." He smiled and shoved me; "Race ya!" he yelled, and took off.

A Melody at Sea

The shorebreak sung to me last summer. It taught me - helped me to listen. Words and time affect each other's existence. Language evolves with time and time is defined by our understanding of language. We're pinned somewhere between, waiting for the waves to come through. (They always do.)

You can feel this out there on the ocean. Or you can feel it anywhere, really.

Communication transcends many different forms. Sentences. Equations. Surfboards and graffiti. All are a product of thought manifested somewhere in the harmony of universe; delivered however and whenever we choose to listen.

German, Italian, French. Sign language. Cave scripture. The Scientific Method. Morris code. Java. HTML. Ccs. Python. The Key of C Sharp. Snares on the attack equalizer.

There's a melody that we can learn to read.

As time proceeds, language evolves. It swells like sets in the ocean. Up and down, up and down. Sometimes rough, sometimes calm. The more it develops, the deeper our collective perception of time goes. We are creatures made out of circles.

I bet you feel it too.

Even though you can't explain it, you hear it singing and you know the words. You remember the key signature and tempo. The hooks and high hats. They're all yours, every time. If you close you eyes and lay flat on the earth, you can feel the gravity pulling at you, burning from within your soul.

I am no different. I am human too. Somehow I've learned to harness it when I float around on the sea.

She rises and falls and soaks in tides like the rest of us. She aids my words and my time like a verse in 3-4, catching me on that thick backbeat with the woosh of the waves. Up there in the sand, language spews from my fingertips like a jellyfish, floating with rhythmic mocean compelled by an eclecticity that's always going. It pumps melody into my heart and I cannot control its tempo. I cannot rewrite its tone.

But I can sing along. I can feel the circle of fifths in every tubed barrel, foaming at the mouth of land and sea.

Out there, I realize the truth that there are no truths. Just listening to what I see and adding to what I'll never truly know. The future is predetermined by my present.

The ocean is me and I am it. Her frequencies resonate my sternum and my toes. A cheerful third eye to read the clock with. Time becomes everything and nothing in the heart of my melodic universe. I hear it nightly - my sheets coated with sand and my hair salted to the pillows. I am words. I am time. I'm but a humble melody at sea.

So Full Our Hearts

Dawn patrol, the morning after a show (the Lonely Biscuits at Asbury Lanes, back when they were a 4-piece and it was still called Asbury Lanes). She's asleep on our bedsheet beside me - couldn't wait for the sun to come up any longer.

We're sitting in the sand where the tide going out meets the one coming in and the waves zipline into each other like a jacket. Over by the jetty; waiting, smiling, laughing.

Finally, a sun sprouts from the horizon and I nudge her. "Here it comes," she says, groggy-eyed and salty. A beamy orange shorebreak portals us passed the humming inlet buoy, a distant bell, a beacon of low-tide, signaling out to our closest star.

"Those clouds back there are crazy!" she smiles again and takes a deep breath. "Don't you just love the smell of low-tide?"

Seussville clouds pillow at the back our heads.

"I do," I say.

She lays back down once the sun turns white. I continue to gawk at the mocean of waves, one after another, after another, after another. A big one, some small ones, two big ones, more small ones. Mother nature's pulse.

The sand beneath me begins to warm, a new opportunity in the pillar of day. My third eye stands tall. Love and air soak into my beard, soon wet with impulsive revelation. I am the universe.

A new light; the same star; inspirational matter; so full our hearts.

Dawn Patrol

I was on the t-rocks at the end of the jetty when I realized exactly where I needed to be. It was just before dawn on a Thursday. 6:17am. Summertime in full bloom with an approximate 71 degrees. I was 20 and still rode a skateboard.

The sunrise helped get me there too; cresting out over swells of golden blues and greens and shimmering in the teals as if it were winking at us. The face. A person. An entity of light molecule penetrating our eyes and lungs like god.

Breathe in, breathe out.

"Let's go already!" His voice echoed up the stairs like footsteps. My brother, at a fresh 18, had energy like a bullet.

New Jersey seemed like the whole world. Manasquan was it's meager capital.

On the rare occasion where I had off from work and the forecast predicted a clear sunrise, I struggled waking up. Normally, I would have just surrendered back to bed after another vain alarm. I'd seen the sky steep from fire to honey and white several hundred times. My mom used to take us to the beach when we were younger and she was an artist.

Today was different though. I was motivated. I was alive. Blake had off from work. So when 4am rolled around, I had my very own *human* alarm clock that smelled like salt water and sunscreen. My eyes found focus on the long, dready hair, dangling over me like a driftwood chandelier. "G'morning, Sunshine," he grinned. He was already in his board shorts. "Time-ta wake up."

"Dude, do you ever shower? You reek... what time is it?"

"Four O' Five, bro! Patrol don't sleep in!"

My brother and I tried to keep tradition alive. We liked to go to the inlet at the end of the beach to watch the sun come up. *But only* when we had off of work together. Otherwise, you'd only find us up there if the swell was good. Sometimes we'd surf, other times we'd drink coffee and eat pork roll sandwiches. No matter what, we grew as human beings.

"Alright, gimme a minute," I said, disheveled and incognizant of what I was about to discover. "I'll meet you downstairs."

"Sure thing, brosef." He turned and left, humming Sublime's "What I Got" to himself down the stairs.

I shook my head and put on some boardies, envious of his radiant energy.

Keys. Bikes. Coffee. Breakfast sammies.

Without waves, we were the only ones there. And that was fine. The sand was cool; salty air - invigorating. I felt something swelling in my heart anyway. Even though it was quiet, the lapping water pockets brought solace alongside our home jetty. The sweeping tractor lights were visible from the north end too, patrolling at dawn.

Breathe in, breathe out.

My brother, after finishing his P.E.C., tore off his shirt and immediately dove into the water. I started walking towards the t-rocks, still pecking at mine. He body-surfed in the mid-tide mush for a few rounds, and then I gave up watching to head towards the other end of the jetty. Further out beyond the shorebreak.

You could feel it coming. That face. The sun. The sentient life of a new day.

It was calm. The sky started to steep and I felt it blossom at the pit of my stomach. The air was motionless. Boat horns signaled between distant tides and buoys chimed a few hundred yards out. The landscape reminded me of one of my mom's paintings hanging in her basement studio - our "Sea-Level Studio" as she called it.

It struck me; *this is where she found inspiration.* The early morning trips suddenly made sense. I felt it in my blood and my lungs too. That salty antidote.

Out on the t-rocks, I balanced myself from falling as I lobbed shells at the same seagulls who tried swiping the last bites of my sandwich.

"Don't hit them!" yelled Blake, climbing up out of the water onto the signal platform. "Danny hit one with a rock once and the police gave his dad a summons!"

"Good! They're rats with wings!"

"Pure evil," he laughed in consent, holding back shivers and waiting for the sun like me.

Breathe in, breathe out.

I stood on the highest rock I could find so that I could see the sun's forehead poke out over the remote flatness. I wanted to feel the first light. Something about it wasn't like the other days.

"Don't fall." Blake hopped over to the same ledge as me.

"Thanks, *dad.*"

"Hey no problem," he smirked. "Here it comes!"

I wondered if this was how people on the west coast felt when they watched the sunset. Did they notice the invisible hairlines collapsing into horizon? Did they feel connected to the universe? Did they mock their brother in signs of affection? Because that's what I saw. That's what I noticed: a huge face whose nose hairs spewed up over the horizon, exhaling wavelengths of spectrum into the atmosphere like a prism. It felt human.

Breathe in, breathe out. I turned, heading over towards the platform.

"Where are you going?" Blake asked.

I looked at him and then back at the horizon and decided I could never replace the sunrise with a sunset. I'd never be able to call California home, even if that seemed like where everyone else around here wanted to go. I didn't need to see the face in the sky sink and drown in dying sunshine. I wanted to see it's birth. It's life. It's first breaths. As many times as I possibly could before I die. Even if I was tired.

"Nowhere," I said as I hopped off. "I'm not going anywhere."

I leapt from rock to rock, back towards the sand as the sun kissed the flesh on my back, reminding me how lucky I was to call this place home.

"Okay," he shrugged. "I'll race you!"

I nodded and shouted "GO!" He glanced at the peeking face for one more brief moment, climbed down onto a t-rock, and dove right into a deep pool of water, swimming towards shore. I paused for a second too, distracted by the sun's face. The hairline was dancing. It doodled up over the distant cargo freighters, painting everything in pinks and yellows like a Jay Alders piece. I smiled to myself and went back slowly. He beat me but it didn't matter. My heart found triumph in the small ribbons of hope and warm weather. I had newly opened eyes... and the keys to the house.

Pork Roll vs. Taylor Ham

The smell of summer crept at our ankles with the shorebreak, sending shivers up our salty calves. The water was still cold. Memorial Day weekend approached rather quickly this year, after what felt like an eternal winter. Flocks of bennys migrated south as the weather warmed, sparking articles in the Asbury Park Press debating whether it was "taylor ham" or "pork roll."

(*It's pork roll.*)

I remember seeing the line at Bar-A the Tuesday night prior. It was up past the train tracks - something only usually seen around Memorial Day, 4th of July, or Labor Day. Natalie and I laughed at the morons who would be spending more on their cover charge than we would for an entire meal at Taco Tuesday on the patio of 10th Ave Burrito. The $7 buckets were just a little sumthin-sumthin extra.

"Did you think they'll ever learn?" asked Natalie, riding past a group of fresh 21-year-olds struggling to walk in high heels around the potholes and puddles.

"Someday," I smiled. "Just like we did."

"I wasn't like *that*!" she said proudly, pointing to a girl wearing some ribbon for a top.

"Shit, I hope not." I laughed. "But we were stupid too at that age. It was only a few years ago."

"And that was enough."

We crossed over 15th, 12th, and 10th and pulled up to the jam-packed bike rack. Summer was officially here. The locals knew what was up.

"Let's lock over here to this tree," I said.

Inside, we asked to be sat under our favorite waiter, Gary. He always tried to help us out - even through the slower winter months when the restaurant lost their seasonal liquor license. They only recently obtained their year-round. Usually he hooked us up with some chips and guac or some leftover Mexican cheesecake. But every once in awhile, he'd spot us a round. Those were the best nights.

"We should try to find some fireworks this weekend," Natalie said.

I pulled out my phone and started scrolling. "Way ahead of you. I have a list going."

Gary came up to the table and set down a bucket of beers. "Hey guys," he said. "Long time, no see. How've you been? Can I get you started with your first round?"

Natalie orders chicken and I go with my usual first: chorizo.

"Okay cool," he said. "Holler if you need anything."

"So Thursday is Point Pleasant, which is a bit far. Friday is Bradley. Avon is Saturday. Belmar is Sunday and Asbury claimed Monday."

"Weird," she chimed in. "Doesn't Asbury usually have Saturday?"

"Maybe for July 4th?"

Our tacos come out and we put in for a second round. This time she orders the chorizo and I went with steak.

"Can you believe the *Asbury Park Press*?" asked Natalie with a mouthful. She took a swig of beer and kept going; "This 'pork roll' or 'taylor ham' crap?"

"I know, right!"

"I mean, who in their right mind calls it 'taylor ham'?"

We both knew the answer to that question. The same people lined up around the block for Beat the Clock. The same people who sit on the beach all day, don't clean up their trash, and then bitch about having to pay for a daily badge. (*They're not from around here.*)

"Don't get me started."

"I just wish that 10th Ave would get on board and make a pork roll taco already!"

"Gary!" I yelled, "We have a suggestion!"

He came over to the table and politely laughed at the same joke he's probably heard a thousand times since the article's release. "I've been saying that for months!"

We put in another round of tacos and ordered margaritas.

"R.F.G.'s?"

Natalie couldn't help herself and said, "I feel like you don't even know us anymore."

"What am I becoming?!" Gary laughed. "Worst waiter ever." He winked and walked away towards the table of college-kid guidos in bro-tanks and hairgel pre-gaming for Beat the Clock or D'Jais or whatever.

I gestured at them and muttered, "Do you think they know they can't get in wearing bro-tanks?"

"Of course not," said Natalie. "But who cares? Let's finish these and head up to the beach for the sunset."

"Deal!"

Our last round of tacos came and went slower than the others. I usually tap out after four rounds but Natalie can barely handle three so I called it quits for the sake of love. We finished our margaritas, people-watching the sore thumbs, and over-tipped Gary because it'd been awhile since our last Taco Tuesday excursion.

On the way up to the beach, I imagined what a pork roll taco would consist of while Natalie made jokes about the *Jersey Shore* wannabes. The sun felt warm on our backs, the bike ride pulsing at minimal speed while everything felt right again. Winter can be so long around here. Sometimes all it takes is that little scent of summer and some tacos.

On the Jetty

Out on the jetty, things make sense. There's some sort of chemical reaction in your brain that takes place between the warm rocks glazed in sunlight, the salty air sponging your lungs, and the cawing gulls that really just triggers your neurons. The water seeps through cracks around you; whirling and whooshing like one of Kerouac's *Big Sur* poems. One where the world seems to finally slow down enough so you can eNJoy the sun on your face and remember what it feels like to be human. I always close my eyes. You want to wander out further but you know the t-rocks get slippery out there and you definitely don't want to fall in when the water's this cold. Not without your wetsuit, at least. It's okay though. This is not your first time climbing on the jetty. This is not your first time glued to the ocean. This is not your first time feeling human. You are exactly where you need to be and everything makes sense.

Ocean Ave Anxieties

As I cruise down Ocean Ave with the wind at my back, I am faced with what first feels like a typical morning. It's a Saturday in mid-June; some clouds but mostly sun; and the solacing smell of ocean licks my nostrils only the way home can. People flock towards the sand with strollers and beach chairs, ready to fully eNJoy their weekend. The last of the morning joggers are thinning out as the sun is almost high noon, producing more warm vitamin D than prefered for beach exercise. A line pokes out of Playa Bowls and protrudes up the sidewalk and down the corner of 8th Ave. It puts a smile on my face, some pride for small local business creasing with the wrinkles of my already sun-burnt face. But surely enough, as I'm nearing the rising bridge before Avon, that pride fades to anxiety. I become engulfed in financial burden. Student loans, car payments, phone bills, a mortgage, and an engagement ring. *What am I to do? How can anyone truly enjoy their weekend with these thorns at their side? Why haven't I come up with an idea as successful as Playa Bowls to help break the societal ball and chain clasped around my ankles?* All I want to do is forget work and money and "quality of life" and enjoy my damn bike ride. Instead, my recursive mind decides to prick me with the apparent "norms" of 21st century adulthood. I immediately recognize a need to meditate but, of course, there's yardwork to be done. These clouds will soon fall thick upon 4pm - a 50% chance of

T-storms. Welcome to New Jersey. *What are you doing, Glen? Focus. Recalibrate. Reset. These anxieties aren't real. Breathe in, breathe out. Repeat. Ride your bike. Do your work.* Then, later that afternoon, I reclaim my present with the sun at my back and stress beyond my shoulders. I somehow find solace in the tide at my toes and an incorrect weather forecast. My hair is salty. The waves woosh therapeutically. I paid my bills. The yard work is done. Happy Hours are on queue and I have a book at my side. The beach called to me, begging to calm down, to be understood. To be present. So I kept going. With the ocean in my veins, I kept going.

Heavy Hearts and Sunscreen

The sky was ripe. Doughy. Pale. Covered in a salty haze. It helped us relax and breathe better. According to the solstice, it was officially summer, though you'd never think, as the air was still springtime chilly. Our hearts were heavy so we brought hoodies and sunscreen just in case.

Dawn spoke to us in a language only her and I were familiar with. One we knew sitting in the sand, warming our skin with rising sun, preparing for a long day ahead. Books stowed for easy-access, water bottle caps locked tight. Phones in little baggies to keep the sand out. Salt crusted our hair and flesh like fishermen. Our flipflops were near-by in case we needed them for the restrooms. We were full force, a summertime dawn patrol, listening to the waves and gulls with eager, young souls ready to inhale some sun. The water was cold but we went in anyway.

Jen and I needed this. We longed for a higher purpose, craving a day to simply sit and reflect, and be awake before the sun comes up without having to go to work. "I can just breathe better up there," she said over her coffee. "Let's spend the day."

My spine was stiff too. She saw the echoes of man from the backyard, pasted to the side of the soft moon like papier-mache.

"Ok," I smiled.

"Good. Let's go up after coffee."

We packed a bag, including the snacks and the water, the books, sunscreen and speakers. Dew coated our bike seats. Silence hung in the air like fog; traffic not yet awake, barely visible in the fresh light of day. Adrenalines seeped through our veins, readying us for an awakening the closer we got to the beach.

"I feel it already," she said, slinging her chair over her shoulder.

"Me too, babe. Me too."

In the Backyard

In the backyard whispers float about the stillness of air like balloons. Creatures sing with dusk and burn off remaining energy by chasing each other from branch to branch. Even distant traffic attempts to distort what the universe is trying to say; yet somehow, nature remains louder for those who can properly focus.

If you listen close enough, the trees will tell you. "We are the veins of earth," one says. "Balance is our axis to reality."

"Yes," says the one wrapped in ivy. Her limbs float with wisdom. "We reach for warmth and knowledge."

Strange that she points this out, because I only notice upon looking at them upside down. They grow in both directions.

"The leaves are lingerie," giggles the stubby one next to the shed. He seems immature.

Had I not been tired and distraught from work, I'd have been more inclined to question the absurdities of talking trees. But my mind is toast. "Oh," I say. "That makes sense - so maples don't like to strut their curves?"

"We don't 'strut,'" blurts the prissy one. "We sway." And she waves back and forth in the absence of breeze as though at a beach-rock concert.

"My apologies," I say.

They stare down at me, waiting, wondering if I am like them; if I am from the earth too. I don't know what to do or say so I sway back and forth, my arms above me, toes rooted deep into the ground like dirt, realizing I will one day decompose like them.

"The little one does well," laughs the meaty oak several lots down. "Let us dance." His voice bellows between shingles and fencing.

And so we dance.

Then reality rushes back in: dogs' barking and train horns firing as it creeps North. Birds grow louder and harmonize with the hum of traffic. I can see the patterns if I close my eyes. They are geometric. I am caught in the melody of nature, lost in universe, surfing vibrations heading somewhere else, riding a wave I am unable to bail from. One that will bring me exactly where I'm going and where I need to be. Listening to the trees in my backyard.

Dune Grass and Lightning Bugs

We used to catch lightning bugs on a small patch of grass that we had by Stockton Lake. They would sprout around 830-9 o'clock at night from the thick areas around the dune grass. Sometimes, if we were good, and dad had a cold beer while supervising, he'd let us cross over to the benches across the street to run around. This was before Sandy had sucked them all out into the lake. It was also before the digital boom. So it was *juuust* before all the bennys from up north moved down here; the same ones who never curb their dog and now let their kids wander around aimlessly playing *Pokemon GO*.

I miss that house. I remember the smell of the fresh cut lawn, the dune grass that tripled in size every June. Even the smell of the dead lightning bugs we'd smush on our faces to make 'em glow. Our cousins were always there, some staying for the whole summer. At least before Danny was diagnosed and we moved to Seattle.

My brother and I *knew* all the best lightning bugs came from the dune grass. The big ones were our facepaint. If you hit enough of 'em, your Wiffleball bat would glow too and you could fence around at each other, pretending to be Luke Skywalker or Obi-Wan.

"I am your father," my brother would say when his bat stopped glowing. And he'd run off towards the dunes. Danny would chase him, barely able to run yet, his little legs still developing their muscle memory.

"Alright boys, time to come inside," my dad would yell across the street.

Mom would make us take showers afterwards because we smelled like insectahomicidal maniacs. Otherwise we'd get our sheets dirty.

"But what about the sand mom?"

"A little sand between the sheets never hurt nobody," she'd laugh. "You get used to it, being so lucky to live where we live."

"I wish Danny still lived here."

"Yeah," my kid brother would chime. "Danny was fun!"

"Get some rest, boys. Tomorrow's a big day." She'd flick the lights out and leave.

"Danny's not coming back, is he?" my brother would ask.

"No," I'd say. "He's not."

"Does dad know?"

"I think so."

"Why did he leave?"

"Mom said he was in a better place."

"Oh," my brother would say. "He knew the best lightning bug spots."

"Yeah."

"By the dune grass?"

"That's right."

"Before he got sick."

"Yeah," I'd say.

Sometimes, when I'm in town, I drive by that house and think about that summer; the last one we got to see Danny in color. They still have the porch furniture set up like we did. Even the spot where they found him, face down on the sofa. The small patch of dirt was paved over and housed some jet skis now. But they still had the dunegrass. And I'm sure they still had some pretty awesome lightning bugs at dusk.

A West Wind

A darkness buzzed around the empty space of my kitchen. Flies doomed to die sat on the window sill. "Yes we did," read the text message. It crept through the holes in my screen. "But we thought it was best not to tell you cause you guys are friends and all."

Part of me knew all along, even though I'd never admit it.

"Oh ok," I said.

"I still don't know who told you that. But it was a one time thing. When we first met. Before I even knew you."

"Ok"

She replied quickly after my intentional lack of punctuation, but I didn't read it. I set the phone down and it buzzed a few more times, devouring sunlight like the horizon. Instead, I slunk down the backside of the earth.

Breathe in, breathe out. Repeat.

With an instant, the solar system buckled at my knees, erasing what I thought was my purpose. I felt betrayed. Insignificant. Lost. My soul, my focus, my organic composition; all devoid with the hollow buzz of a few text messages.

Next thing I know, I'm on the front steps of my house, then out by the street, twiddling the business card back and forth between my fingers, wondering if I'd just thrown away an entire month's income.

"Maybe I was wrong," I said to the curb.

The image wouldn't get out of my head. I looked at the sunset and saw him and her instead. Time pinched at my nerves; pulse data leaking through my veins like binary. Birds swam from branch to branch. Newlyweds walked their dogs. Even the fireflies had someone to die with. The sunset destined me to a darkness of solitude, fated to explore the universe solo. I was losing it.

Just breathe.

That's when I heard it calling. Just like it always does.

Sometimes she howls, other times she cries like a newborn. Today was more of a *psst, psst* like a bug caught in the west wind, scampering to stay alive, clasping at any piece of solid matter it can before inevitably getting sucked out to sea.

I was that fly. I was summoned by means of a higher consciousness, one capable of changing shapes and colors. The ocean called for me - beckoning in my misery - destined to dance in saltwater and soul. She was alive. And I listened.

I grabbed my longboard, still barefoot, cruised the 7 blocks up to the boardwalk ignoring the present around me. I moved past things I normally wouldn't.

"Hi there Allen!" said Mike as I rode by his coffee shop.

"Beers tonight?" laughed Bill, our neighbor on 6th.

"Allen, dear, are you and Melissa still in for board game night?" asked Joanne.

I kept going. Right past all of them, all sitting on their porch as if nothing mattered.

It was dusk, and the evening joggers had about called it quits. There were no cars for me to jump in front of. *Maybe she's not,* I thought. *Am I full of shit?*

Psst, psst. Psst. Psst.

I left my phone at home with my heart, running circles through my mind like razor blades. Hell, I don't even know why I asked. Curiosity, I guess - shadows of a buzzing past that would not let go. They picked at the back of my eyelids like parasites. I was weak.

Psst, psst. Psst. Psst.

And then I made it. My feet sunk right into the summer sand, still holding the sunlight from hours ago. Solace found me by a shorebreak too foamy to drown in.

It wasn't even the fact that she slept with him. The sand helped me see that. It was before we even knew each other. What burned more was that she hid it from me after introducing us years ago. No "Just So You Know" conversation. Even though I *specifically* recall being yelled at and guilted for not having the same kind after introducing Lauren, one of my ex's.

No, I had to stumble upon it based on an observed nonverbal social behavior as witnessed at a party over the weekend. As if my energies were destined to know. She and Justin had been batting eyes all night. It really knocked my teeth out when I caught her putting her arm around his waist. Remnants of Genghis Khan huddled at the back of my skull like fog pumping testosterone into my thought pores.

It should've been my arm. My waist.

I sat down near the water, absent-minded and lacerated, my guts spilling out into the sand like a whale carcass. The ocean was quiet. Small shorebreak waves yipped at the ankles of toddlers and fishermen; weak and slow like me. Time skipped again. The sky bleeds out and fades purple and dark, forcing everyone to pack it in. Salty air lined my lungs and helped the water settle me.

Psst, psst. Psst. Psst.

"It's okay," she said, lapping at my toes. "She didn't mean to hurt you."

"I know," I whispered. "I know.

Boathouse Chips

"How's the weather over there?" she says.

I'm staring at her over some classic Boathouse chips. One of them looked like the shape of New Jersey so I Instagram'd it to distract myself from saying what I really wanted to say. *Just shut up about it!*

"It's a bit loud," I respond. Pat Roddy's cover band was setting up.

"You haven't said anything since the conversation about… well, you know."

"Yeah." I don't mean to be short. But I'm an introvert so sometimes I can't help it. It just happens.

She goes on talking about how she doesn't like being alone. Which I can relate to. I'm not really listening; too busy trying to get the image of her and Justin mauling each other out of my head.

I don't like being alone sometimes either. But other times I can smile at the thought of living a life of solitude in a small beach bungalow in Lavalette or Ortley. Is that part of the human condition? I'm sure part of that is somewhere on Maslow's hierarchy of needs.

Somehow she ends up on next month's Cape May trip. "What do you think?" she says, "I can make the reservation for us tomorrow morning."

"Sure that sounds good."

She puts her hands down and looks at me with that face like she doesn't get me. She's been an extrovert her whole life. I knew this going into the relationship.

"What's wrong?"

"You already know."

"Seriously, Allen? It was six years ago. I didn't even know you. Justin and I went on a few dates. So what?"

I took a gulp of my beer and set it down slowly, trying to think of what to say. But socially awkward things like this always left me empty-headed. "I just need a minute, okay?"

"You've had 3 days! God, Al. I've eaten half my panini."

She hadn't. There were only a few bites missing.

"It's not like we still feel that way. We tried and it didn't work. Now we're friends." She paused, took a sip of appletini and looked at me. "And now you guys are friends. We just thought it was information that you didn't need to know."

"So this is how I find out? Making assumptions based off of your drunken behaviors at a party last weekend? For fuck's sake, Melissa. I'd rather you have been honest about it upfront than seeing him put his hand on your waist like that. You know I'm a Behavioral Therapist, right? I have a master's in psychology and human behavior."

She shakes her head and says, "I have to use the restroom," and excuses herself from the table.

I sit in a crowded bar, alone and irate over something that means absolutely nothing in the grand scheme of things. I eat my burger. Drink my beer. She comes back 5 minutes later ready to fire. But I beat her to the punch.

"I'm sorry," I say. "I overreacted. I'd just you rather be upfront and honest about these sorts of things. Otherwise it feels like you're hiding from me."

Her shoulders sink, re-organizing her monologue. "Me too," she says. "I didn't mean to hurt you. I just don't know how to tell you I've slept with someone upon you first meeting them."

I laugh. "Well you don't have to do that. But if it comes up, please don't keep it from me. I'd rather not find out through my own assumptions."

There was a silence. "You know, like you asked me to do with Lauren?"

"Okay." She smiles. "Now can we drop it?"

"Please!" I finish my beer and empty my lungs with a long, quiet sigh of relief.

The ring was being set this weekend. Monday I'd be picking it up while she was at work. I'd call out sick, take the train to Red Bank to meet with Mr. Bauman and make the final payment. Next month was it. Do or die. Anxiety brewing at maximum levels. She still had no clue.

"So Cape May huh? What made you suggest that for our first-date-a-versary?"

"Dunno," she smiles after another sip of appletini. "Thought it'd be nice."

"It will be," I say. "It's just what we needed."

Life Lessons of *Pokemon GO*

I was biking up to the beach one hot and sweaty afternoon when a kid on a skateboard barrelled into me at the 10th Avenue red light outside of Surf Taco. He was on his phone. We both fell over.

"*Pokemon GO*," he shrugged, not even breaking for eye contact. "Sorry."

He was tall and lanky, maybe a year or so out of high school, and his red hair poked out of a raggedy Billabong hat like overgrowth. I felt his ambivalence radiating from the raw contusions.

"No worries," I laughed. "Be careful with that, man."

He sulked behind the screen. "Yeah."

"Did you get him?"

"No, it got away."

He finally looked up and I smiled.

"Bummer."

"Yeah," he said. "Hey do you know where the gym is around here? I can't find it."

"No, sorry. I'd guess somewhere by the beach? You should really try to be more aware, ya know. Don't let that game consume you. It's not real."

"Yeah, thanks." He brushed himself off and went east across Main Street, face back buried in his phone.

Part of me hoped I'd gotten through to him. A profound life-lesson, reminding him to alway be present. I envisioned myself a role model; a teacher of sorts. You know the ones. The mentor-type roamers coming along every so often, offering wisdom and advice to the future generations of society with thorns in their sides. The kind of man whose stature poised confidence and virtue; he smokes cigars and reads books no one's ever heard of, drinking morning tea and evening whiskey on his porch. People come to listen to his stories with bellies full of curiosity. They learn. They laugh. They leave.

I shook my head and resumed my ride up to the ocean.

What did I know? The kid cost me a Pikachu wandering around by the median. And the gym wasn't anywhere near Main Street *or* 10th Ave. *Noobs.*

The Ocean is a Person

There's something so human about her, the way she can be. She's like you or me - floating tides in, floating tides out; mood swings and fits of laughter. Crashing, splashing, and mashing.

So what if she has a higher sodium count? Who cares if there's more omega than anyone knows what to do with? No matter how you see, she's a person. The way she laughs, the way she cries. The way she gets dressed up nice when it's cold outside. Sometimes, when the sun hits her just right, there's a glitter far beyond her own smile, even when it's flat. And don't get me started on those little-bikini rough-riptide days.

Sometimes I drive by in my Jeep just to let her know that I'm still here, still listening from Ocean Ave; windows down far enough to absorb some salty air. Other times I skip shells over the lowtide shorebreak in July.

She knows. She won't forget. I can't let her. Her heart might be bigger than mine, and more fluid, but that doesn't mean we aren't in love. I will always answer when she calls. I will always dance across sandbars and surf the double overhead during local summer. Always.

She understands me like no one does. When I need to vent, she'll listen. When I'm lost, she'll bring me home. That's what I love about her. She's the reason I get out of bed on overcast days. And skip out of work early when there are waves. She's the air in my lungs. The blood in my heart. The salt still crusted in my beard. She gets it.

Without the ocean, I am not human. Just another lost soul, wandering existence in hopes to find whatever it is we live for.

Where It All Makes Sense

Meet me where the shadows are stretched long and high tide licks at your ankles with shorebreak dusk.

Where the horizon is flat and birds soar above coastlines like ambient soundwaves.

Where whitecaps are painted gold and distant swells bathe in velvet and silk.

Come find me where the jetty cuts back enough for our souls to recharge at the edge of the universe.

Where the ocean glows like a soulmate knotting the strings behind your heart.

Where the nearby traffic isn't as loud or as happy as the foam at your feet.

Let's aim to call where gulls' wings flutter purple and orange and the sky that touches the ocean is no longer blue, but hazed in warm froth instead.

Where the inlet buoy beacons crews and captains of tankers and yachts.

Where chemtrails run parallel to the horizon and all who wander are far from being lost.

Find yourself where the children's laughter ziplines through wet sand and eons of shorebreak.

Where the sunshine and salty mist of tides remind you of home.

Where life leaks out your pores like sap and salt and the only thing you wish to accomplish is to figure out what it all means.

Yeah, I'll find you at home, where you know it all makes sense.

In the Backyard (pt. 2)

We caught the sun in the palms of our hands that night, sprawled out along pockets of grass and distant trees. Its amber light seeped through their trunks and licked our eyelids like bits of stardust. July had finally found us. Like it always does.

"KSSHHT. Roger that. We've found what're we're looking for," she declares in her captain's pose.

I salute, "Yes ma'am!" and toss her back into my freshly trimmed lawn, then onto the blanket while the woodlands dance.

A projector dresses the side of our house with silhouette pixels. It's warm enough for barefeet. And the laughter howls from deep inside our bellies.

"That's not how it goes!" she says. "But look over the ocean. Look at those stars!"

"My moon, my sun, my stars," I say, pointing to each of them, the stars heliotroped over the horizon. "Count to three."

"One, two, three, and *be together*," she sings, stumbling on her smile.

Another 7 grooves into our hearts like glass. And we melt. Vibrations; beading energy at my brow;

stocked full of happiness, laughter, and vitality. Her sunglasses are buried in her hair like a headband, shaken in the beat of it all. The universal pulse, gardening my heart by the sea.

"I love that song," she says.

"Me too."

"Gimme your phone," she yanks it from my pocket, lint and all.

And as if they already know; "Shall we sway," whisper the trees. I nod. They waft in the breeze.

She searches for The Green on Spotify; all the entities of light tumulting, mirroring our expressions at this very moment of space and time. We become the trees, the birds, the earth. We live together. We dance together. We decompose together. In the backyard.

Frequencies

You crawled out of bed at 8am and felt tired. Tired of work, tired of money, tired of your life - though you'd never admit that to anyone. Except maybe yourself.

At least Parade Day was here. The first Sunday of every March. The one day a year where we could tune those things out and drink like we were in college again. Like Ryan was still breathing.

"I'm sorry," you mutter to the mirror, wiping Jameson dribble from your chin, not even sure who you're apologizing to anymore.

This pang opened your ribcage 9 years ago, to the very day. You watched as he drank himself into a coma. Then death. And *you know* you know better, but you never forgave yourself. Even though it *probably wasn't* your fault.

Your guests show up around 9:30 and we have hearts like Hemingway. You're on the porch with your notebook and a giant cup of what you tell us is coffee. Yours is Bukowski. The music goes on and we join you so you don't have to hide it anymore. Everyone drinks all day, as if we'd already forgotten about him. As if his frequencies were silent.

You were both sophomores in college, home for the weekend with all the other shore kids. He wore his green flannel. You had the suspenders. Some cops found him facedown under the docks behind Kleins. And you could've cut him off after his seventh bump in the stall at Bar-A.

It's okay though. It has to be. We drink and dance and laugh all day long. You are the only one wearing a mask.

"This is what you wanted," you blurt to the puddle of beer on the floor. We pretend not to hear you.

Most of us clung to new dreams, calling out of work on Monday just to try and feel alive again. To remind us of our human. Others would go into work anyway, pretending they had their shit together. They'd find theirs face-down in the toilet stall.

Not you though. You found yours scowling old pictures on Ryan's Facebook page after the party, half-asleep and half-empty. Your bedside light is on and the TV flickers the other room, glittering party cups and bottle caps with bits of his memory. Everyone else is gone and you're alone. Your heart clugs like an overloaded washing machine and you find shapes in the shadows that look like waves.

Strange, you thought, *how the ocean comes **to you***.

Your think about your sudden insignificance. How his frequencies can trigger your senses, even after all these years. Your place in the universe becomes clear. Like we conspired against you, just to remind you that it's okay to be happy. Even when you have to recalibrate.

Up At Night

I couldn't sleep so I sat up on my porch listening to the ocean. The shorebreak leaked through darkness like radiation and I easily surrendered.

Stress lined my blood cells in restive apprehension and all my eyes wanted to do was peel themselves apart. If you asked my husband, he'd tell you it was because of work. But that's only because that's what I told him.

Ask me and I couldn't give you an honest answer. I knew I needed something, had no idea what it was. *Were my boys happy? Did the dog have enough food to last the week? Did I remember to pay the cell phone bill this month?*

Waves were always louder at night.

How much was in the savings account again?

Something about the darkness helped sound travel better. It echoed between houses and cars like gravity and settled somewhere between the crevices of earth. One or two deep breaths and you were good to go. Even from the porch.

So I tried. I sat quietly, absorbing the slush and woo of every set. *Could the be that madness Kerouac was talking about?* The salty air went in and out of my lungs like a slow revolving door. Molecules of time and sound. In and out. In and out.

I felt better.

Distant cars hummed by, sometimes a train. My neighbor left his porch light on again. *Should I tell him?*

The furniture was coated with condensation. *Only now I realize these things?*

The stars were fogged and heavy. *Am I that aimless?*

Breathe in. Breathe out. *Do I matter?*

My dog, Dex, groggy-eyed and yawning, came out to join me; proceeding to nap up across my feet. He was warm with sleep.

"Rub it in, why dontcha?" *What I'd give to trade brains with you.*

And then I felt it. The meaning of it all. The secret to everyone's happiness, whether or not they even knew they had it. The galaxies of atoms squished between our souls and species; our singularities thumped like a heartbeat. Dex didn't know. Or maybe he did. I'd become the fly on the wall; up at night in the emptiness of space.

I am me. We are we.

That daunting sliver of time, merely my past, present, and future. A cocoon of our perceived existence, somewhere along the sea where I'd lost what I even was in the first place.

My husband, my boys, my job. My brief slice of life, breathing cold salty air on my porch along the coastline of New Jersey. I was everything I'd ever experienced, packed neatly into meaty mass of conscious stardust. My heart was pure, tension was temporary, and I could smell the ocean.

And that was close enough for me.

February Fire

Watching the sunrise in your rear-view is depressing. It goes against everything we are as an evolved species, running away from our new risings. At least that's what Shane's heart told him every morning. *Going to work for 80% of our lives just to pay the bills and keep living?* Seemed backwards. A figment of someone's greedy, corrupt imagination.

He drove West on 195 as usual, leaving the coastline sunrise behind him like a bag of rocks. It grew colder as February crept in, his bones reminding him of the broken heater in that '03 Altima. Work would be long today. Several meetings on schedule, plus his annual review and the leftover paperwork from the day before. At least seeing Warren, the toothless forklift operator, would help get him through it. He always had the _best_ dirty jokes.

As overwhelmed as he felt, Shane tried not to let missing the sunrise bother him too much. There'd be more. Besides, he had a plan. It was **THE** Friday. The tanks were set to blow at precisely 6 o'clock. As long as everyone left on time (which they always did), no one would get hurt.

Jacob, his station neighbor, had no idea that he'd be the one to take the fall for this. He was unaware that Shane had taken some access codes from the binder left sitting on his forklift.

No one would suspect the quiet, introverted kid from Bradley Beach.

Jacob Jordon, on the other hand, well, he was the loud mouth from Howell, always talking about how this was just an "in-between" job for him. They'd pin it on him without second guessing it.

And so when he pulled into the parking lot, greeting Nick, the security guard, he held onto his lungs like they were the building that'd soon be on fire.

Late Night Roadtrip

On a Wednesday night in April Alex found himself hovering over a crummy cup of diner coffee with his new girlfriend, Kira. He'd just finished writing a paper for American Lit a few hours ago and Kira wanted to get out of the dorm, adhering to the "roommate code."

"I can't believe her," whined Kira. "A text would have been fine! Just one. It would've taken three seconds."

"Shannon is usually good about that, no?"

"Yeah!" laughed Kira. "She must have really liked him."

"I mean, Brett *is* a good-lookin dude," joked Alex.

Kira shot him a glare.

"Too soon? I'm sorry," he smiled.

Alex sipped his coffee and picked at what was left of the cheesecake.

"I just need to get out of here for a while," said Kira.

"I hear that! That paper had me by the balls. Dr. Shaw can be an asshole about deadlines - I'm just glad I got it done on time. Last time he wouldn't accept it because I submitted it five minutes after midnight!"

"I believe it. I had him last semester for Medieval Lit. Barely finished with a C." She sipped her iced tea, no lemon wedge. "Hey - do you wanna drive home for a bit?"

"Now? It's Wednesday. Almost..." he looked at his phone. "Eight -"

"Yeah, why not?"

"It's almost 8:30. That's a 45 minute drive."

"And?"

"I mean," he trailed off and took the last gulp of coffee. "I have class tomorrow morning at 8am."

"Oh don't be such a vagina," spat Kira, only half-joking. "I just need to escape for a bit. Hear the waves. Touch the sea. Doesn't that ever happen to you?"

Alex thought for a minute. It did. Quite often, actually. He could recall countless times when he was a kid, riding his skateboard up to the beach just to stick his feet in the water. Almost as if it called to him.

"Yeah," he mumbled shamefully.

"So let's go then," she smiled. "You drive there; I'll drive back. I'll even pick up the tab!"

They finished, paid the bill, and stood up to leave - Alex a little more reluctantly than Kira. The drive was long. They left for Point Pleasant; their little hidden abode by the sea. The edge of the world.

Funny enough, Alex and Kira met in college, even though they came from the same high school. The Boro. Ocean County's finest. They knew of each other as teenagers, but didn't *know* each other as teenagers.

"We need a playlist," said Kira.

In the car - that old, dirty, beat-up piece of shit Volvo - she played DJ on a 3rd generation iPod while Alex sped down 195 with TCNJ in the rearview. Kira seemed to already feel better, the closer they got. Alex noticed this change in himself, too. He felt himself able to breathe better as the air became more salty.

"What beach should we go to?" asked Alex.

"Inlet. Duh," said Kira. "That way we can go out on the jetty."

It was clear and unusually warm for April. A humid lull bubbled over the Manasquan Inlet proving the existence of climate change. Immediately upon arrival, both rolled their pant legs up and discarded their shoes as if it were summer.

"Race ya!" yelled Kira, taking off towards the water.

Alex let her go and strolled up past the boardwalk, onto the sand, and down to the water. He watched her dance across the foggy moonlight with a grin on his face. And the second his toes hit the shallow, icy water, everything felt better. Class tomorrow would come and go and the world would keep on spinning. He should've just listened to the ocean in the first place. Sometimes she brought it all back down to earth.

Spring Cleaning (Bikes and Burritos)

At the start of spring my eyes always spit up wind-blown tears in the sharp air. It was just last week; warm enough to break out the bicycle, cold enough to wear socks; allergies about to shift into full gear in the coming days. At dinner, over soup and burritos, we calculated 7's scattered about our surroundings. They've patterned my entire life span and now she's seeing the effects. It radiates beyond my aura. She felt it.

Upon this awakening, we smiled and laughed at the other awkward date-nights around us.

"Do you think that's first date?" She nodded to my six.

"Oh definitely," I said, glancing over my shoulder.

Things are simpler in terms of bikes and burritos. There's time to think. Time to drift. Time to love. Our souls bounce along strings tied together with harmony. The boundaries of work and personal finance float along with the tide; nothing that they are in the grand scheme of things. Balance came to us when it got warm out.

"And the people at the long table over there? That's definitely a fight."

She noticed the angst in the man's eyes. "For sure."

I strapped my GoPro to the bike that night so the memory would become permanent. Years from now, someone might access the file to witness our documented moment. Perhaps our future children. Or grandchildren. But the truth is, that too will one day fade. Material elements, no matter what, end up rotting in the dirt or drifting into space.

"They're like us," she pointed to the people leaving with their doggy bags. "They're happy. This is like their seventh date! It has to be."

I smiled. "Maybe not, but yeah I see that too. They've been through it before. Enough for him to keep his phone on the table the whole time."

Love and happiness though - see, they are immune to rotting in boundaries of time. And there's something about the way the earth tilts back towards the sun that sparks those flames inside of our guts. It changes the fluid levels in our neurological and cardiovascular systems. Gravity tugs at our soul strings like a cool breeze.

Spring brought us the warmth we've known all our lives.

"Does that bother her, you think?"

"No," she said. "She's smiling too much."

Thus, there we were. It was in that afternoon hope which we unlocked the shed and tuned up the bikes. Their gears were as stir-crazy as we'd been. They ached to breathe in the wind of time just as our bellies longed for burritos and soup. Some Friday happy hour sunshine does the body good.

"Well yeah, thanks a lot, by the way. Cause I totally caught your seven symptoms," she laughed. "At first, I thought you were just crazy. But then I saw it. It must've rubbed off on me. Two times I looked at my phone at work today. And you know what times they were?"

I shrugged, still smiling, already cognizant of the answer.

"11:07 and 2:17. Both times to answer texts that you sent me."

"I'm sorry," I said. "It's a plague."

"No. It's a cure. It'll help us tomorrow when we set up the porch furniture."

"I've already got the playlist queued up."

She smiled. "I'm just glad that it's finally here. Winter felt so long this year."

And just like that we drifted into the tide, ready to melt with our clocks. Bikes and burritos were the

only way we knew how to kick off spring cleaning.
Just as long as we wore socks.

Saturday Morning. A Portrait.

Saturday morning. A Portrait. Natural light in the backyard, filtering my caffeinated brain cells. It soaks in through my hair, my clothes, even through the flesh of my eyelids (when they're closed). Grass itching for its first haircut wiggles in the breeze. Iced coffee from Turnstile, resting, periodically sipped, pressuring my heart to reach new bpms.

We'd made it another night. Our floating rock still spinning. Sounds of Spring float with the subtle breeze. Birds chirping. Landscape equipment. Distant 16th Ave traffic.

Tree shadows dance across the patio like the inlet tide. I notice them periodically.

Her eyes glimmer when she opens them to look at me, at what I'm doing. She'll never quite understand what I'm thinking about until she reads this. Even though she could probably take a very good guess. Always writing.

"We should do some yardwork today," she says.

"Definitely," my mouth blurts on its own.

The lines of ivy mock my existence, peaking under and over my fence, teasing me from my neighbor's garage wall. *Thump, thump, thump*, says his hammer. *Chirp, chirp, chirp,* say the birds from his tree.

"But then we go to the beach. That's our prize."

"Deal," she says.

I am a piece of matter with consciousness and enough intellect to experience guilt for not wanting to do yardwork. *Thanks a lot, evolution.* It slumps me at the patio table, not ready to begin chores, not ready to be good at adulting. I want to sit and write and tan my flesh with what little free time from work I actually have. But I don't let that stop me. I get up and go because all I want is to get onto that warm sand. It *is* a Saturday afterall. And life is too short to bitch about it.

Birdwatching

Most people laugh at me when I tell them I enjoy watching the birds from my porch. But I should know better than to drop that line at social functions. Ever since I've been old enough (and $$$ enough) to buy a home, I've enjoyed sitting on my property and watching the birds. Well - nature really. I like to try and experience things that happen when humans aren't around (and sometimes when they are). Everything has personality. Even the trees.

This current home is seaside, just blocks from the ocean **and** the river. So we get a lot of good bird traffic. My shed has some spiders too, but they're not as exciting to watch on the regular, as one would presume. Last season we also had some squirrel problems, but they didn't come back this year, thank god.

"I mean, I don't go all Bear Grylls. But after work. With a nice cup of green tea. Maybe coffee if it's a weekend morning and I get out there early enough. Can't beat it," I explain to the weirdo from Tinder, Tim.

"My thesis was on the mating habits of sea gulls," he said. Everyone else had gone back to the patio table after my bird comment. "Specifically, the Herring."

Monkia glances over to mouth "I'm sorry" with a smile like she didn't mean it.

"Oh?" I ask, because I'm too nice.

"Yeah - I'm a class away from my Masters in Marine Bio," he boasts. "Over there at Monmouth."

"Congratulations," I say.

"Thanks."

I flip a few of the burgers and swig the last sip of beer. Tim, the Tinder guy, goes to get us more from the cooler. Monika is rounding 30 and getting desperate. I get annoyed when Sarah invites her to our things. Every time it's some new goober. The last one brought his unicycle.

Jeff, Caitlin, Sarah, and Monika are sitting at my patio set in the shade. I'm getting jealously burnt in the residual sunshine with Tim and a fresh beer. At least the birds are moving around.

"So what made you choose the ocean?" he asks, readjusting his glasses.

"I'm sorry?"

"Why'd you buy near the ocean in New Jersey? Not much bird life out here where it's densely populated. The best spots are inland, near lakes and ponds."

I nod and flip two more of the burgers.

"Plus, it's pretty expensive," he adds.

The Thursday sun starts to rear and set over the trees on the opposing side of the river. This is my favorite time of day to bird-watch. Feeding time. From my front porch, you could see them skim the water surface for bugs and small fish.

The backyard, though; that was a little different. Less seabirds and more woodland ones with the nearby treelines and all.

Sarah had planned this small get-together to celebrate the 4th of July weekend before all the craziness hits. The bennys usually flood Belmar Friday morning and don't leave until Tuesday. So we try to plan our family parties accordingly, traveling inland for those when we can. The bird-traffic isn't as great, but it's nice to see the variety that Jersey has to offer.

I set the tray of burgers on the table and grab a seat, right next to Tim of course. "These look great," says Caitlin. "And Sarah - that watermelon salad was to die for. You have to give me that recipe."

"It's just watermelon, chopped onions, and feta," she says. "Who woulda thought?"

Jeff reaches in for the first cheeseburger. "Thanks dude," he looks at me. "It's nice to start the weekend low-key like this."

"Definitely," I say. "Do you guys have any other barbeque plans this weekend?"

"My parents have theirs on Sunday usually. Tomorrow we're going to the beach and Saturday is his college buddy's party. Carter, right?" She looks at Jeff. He nods, a huge mouthful restricting him from forming words.

"The beach?" says Monika. "So brave of you."

"I know, I know," says Caitlin. "But we'll be down on 5th ave, so hopefully there won't be as many of them."

"Good luck," I smile.

Tim, the Tinder guy, looks up and says, "Why? What's wrong with the beach on Friday?"

Sarah would later tell me that he's from Freehold and doesn't get it. But I'd pretty much figured that out already.

Jeff chimes in and says, "It's super crowded on holiday weekends. Lot of out-of-towners."

"Ah," says Tim, readjusting his glasses. "Makes sense."

"How bout you two?" asks Sarah.

Tim and Monika look at each other. There's an awkward silence. Monika chews what was already in her mouth. Tim readjusts his glasses again. I take a sip of my beer and lean back, finally able to enjoy the birds talking to each other.

"Not sure," smiled Tim. "This is our first date."

Sarah would later tell me about how she *can't believe* Monika, *can't believe* she brought a Tinder date to a BBQ, *can't believe* Monika hasn't given up on internet dating, *can't believe* she's rushing into things like this, and *can't believe* she hasn't found a nice guy yet.

"Oh," says Sarah. "That's nice! Hope we didn't give you any ideas." She winks at Tim, who I'm sure does not understand her sense of humor yet. "Maybe you guys can catch some fireworks tomorrow night."

"That's a great idea!" says Monika.

Tim eats his burger in silence while the conversation morphs into gardening, then into how the designated hitter is still ruining baseball, and then into a potential bike crawl in September. I feel bad for him momentarily until he reaches *over* Sarah for the ketchup like he's not even listening. *Just ask dude.*

The sun goes down and our solar lights power on. Birds have quieted. Our music echoes off the fence and spills faintly into the neighbor's yard. Monika's sporadic laugh overpowers all of it and floods the street like a muffler so I don't feel too bad. I am good and drunk by this point so I sink back into my chair and watch everyone's personalities as if they were the birds.

"It's already 10," says Jeff.

He sounds worried so Caitlin says, "Okay, I'll call an Uber."

"We should go too," says Monika. "I have work tomorrow morning."

"You didn't take off?" asks Tim, the Tinder guy.

"I took Tuesday," she replies. "Monday night is local night."

The four of them head inside and I reluctantly follow, as I took off both Friday *and* Tuesday. Sarah has fallen asleep in her chair but I'd come back out later to bring her to bed. In the meantime, I helped flock some birds through my house and out into their respective cages.

My Dog, the Bird Killer

My 10lb dog murdered a baby bird this past weekend. When I caught him, the corpse strung between his jaw, he gave me a victorious glare - as if he'd conquered an objective he set for himself as a puppy - his eyes luminous with soul.

One day I'll get those winged monsters. One day.

The following Monday I felt groggy and unprepared for work. Things moved in slow motion and it took three cups of coffee to put my brain back together. All I could see when I closed my eyes was the lifeless pink cardinal between my dog's gnarled teeth.

As a grown man, it's difficult to admit my compassion for the bird, my empathy for the bird's mother who watched as he snapped its neck not seconds after it fell from the tree.

I said something to my fiancee, who then insinuated that I was full of estrogen. *Jersey girls*.

Nature has its way of doing. And, as a human, I accept that. I am okay with it. I am okay with death and dying and my little miniature pinscher being capable of execution. That is life.

My dog, the bird killer, brought emphasis of my own inevitability here along the coastline of New Jersey. Ultimately, that's all there is at the end of the tunnel, no matter how I choose to paint the walls. His murderous teeth flossed with feathers reminded me of that simple truth.

The experience. The journey. The process. Whatever you wish to call it, it's there and it's always surprisingly relentless. Encoded somewhere in my string of fate, it was set that I would spend 20 minutes of my Saturday morning chasing the dog around so he wouldn't choke to death trying to swallow it whole. And that's only after Mama Redbird was shooed from dive-bombing him.

With the next few days came reflection. I thought about our time in this country, on this planet, in this universe. Neurons fired, filling my head with a translucent glimpse of what reality has in store for us. One day you're born, ready to spread your wings and go. Then you take a wrong step, fall out of the nest a little too early, and get consumed by a greater destiny.

Fate is around every corner, waiting to pounce on you while you're learning to fly. The key is not letting that distract you from your desired objective. Sometimes the universe has a different plan.

The Porch

The clouds billowed in from the west, half-stormy, half-marshmallow between bits of sun. It was just recently spring but felt like February between chills. Gardens and florists cursed the groundhog who caused this; when really, it was just the climate change or methane gas or whatever excuse the government scientists were cooking up at the time.

Rachel wasn't coming home until later, and the dog was at her parents for the weekend. "My dad wants to see him. I think it'll cheer him up," she pleaded the week prior.

I knew not why she felt as if she had to convince me, but I wasn't complaining. "Sounds good," I said. It would surely be a relaxing evening of video games, beer, and angry punk-rock playlists on Spotify.

There was a long list of things to do written on the fridge's white-board when I got home from work that night. Laundry, dishes, clean the toilet, take out trash, call Jordan, walk the dog, write cover letter, mail Karen's check. I stood in front of it, breathing patterns onto the glossy cardboard, wishing I could somehow go back to being a kid. *Some of these things would still be on your list, you douche.*

Half-way through the dishes, I noticed the sporadic sunlight spilling onto the porch, calling for me to press pause. Our porch was still in winter mode, so we had the glass panes in. *If I were to hobble over there, I bet it'd be warm enough to pretend,* I thought.

I quickly packed the dishwasher, started it, stared at it, and skipped over the new Blink-182 track and some Crass song that I didn't recognize. I landed on the Dead Kennedys' "Funland at the Beach" and I felt it again. Something hit me in the rib cage only the way summertime sadness would. I knew it was too soon, but sprung out onto the porch anyway, browsing through #DGAF memes on Instagram.

If she calls me, I won't answer. I won't answer, no way. My mind was a blender. Her words echoed endlessly between my head and my heart. An infinite loop of pulpy, apologetic syntax. Reality sinking into my bones like calcium.

The air was chilly, not too wet, and felt right on your skin through the glass. It wasn't too bad. Somehow, people mustered up enough courage to walk their dogs and gave me something to watch besides the screen of my phone. It was warm, but not **that** warm.

"I'm sorry," she muttered, as if it changed anything. "It was a mistake. A one time thing."

Old cotton felt worse in the 6 o'clock overcast sun. It chaffed your skin like the rough side of a sponge. Light spilled through the windows and soaked through my ratty Stone Pony t-shirt, reminding me so. If I closed my eyes tight enough, I could smell the burnt fibers.

"You have every right to hate me."

My heart or my head needed ocean so I opened the window and let some cold air flood in. The waves were distant, but I could make them out, one by one, crashing over each other like the backside of the inlet. It was worth the temperature dip.

My heart was the one who decided to leave the solace of my porch and walk up to the boardwalk. My head and my bones screamed at me when I got there.

It was a mistake. It was a mistake.

The sun sunk faster than I'd planned, so my walk was short-lived. But it was enough salty air to do the trick. I went back to the porch after only fifteen minutes, feeling full.

"A mistake?" I replied. "Mistakes can be erased. Forgiveness is not an eraser."

Her eyes grew watery. "I'll bring Bella to my parents' this weekend. My dad wants to see him. I think it'll cheer him up."

Her shit was boxed and stacked neatly beside the spare bedroom door, just inside the porch. I'd stepped over it a hundred times that morning. But when I got back from the beach, I forgot it was there and stumbled over them stepping in. This, in turn, upset me again so I piled them outside next to the door.

"Sounds good," I said, the last words I'd ever speak to her. "I'll leave your stuff on the porch."

The Bike Path

There is a stretch of pavement that runs through the woods like a spinal cord, winding between trees and highways towards the ocean. Brett and Vinny knew it like the veins in their arms.

They rode bikes on it in the spring and summer; sometimes from Brett's house near Allaire State Park all the way into Manasquan. Other times they'd stop under some of the street lamps near Vinny's to smoke joints on a Wednesday after school. At least, Vinny did. Brett only tagged along for those. He played three sports, one in every season.

Sometime in the late 2000's an offshoot was built, going perpendicular towards the Municipal Complex in Wall. Old timers were offended, being that the original Bike Path was created to replace the long-since-used railways. "'The Edgar Felix Bicycle Path.' That's what the sign says," they'd mutter over early-bird happy hours. "Not 'The Willy Nilly Bike Path'!" Vinny's dad did a really good old-guy voice.

It did not last long, as things never do. Asphalt bleeds when it's cut. It has spirit like anything else.

One summer before college, on this same blacktop, Vinny crumpled his best friend's trust like a paper wad. The very same stretch where Brett decided to leave New Jersey forever. It bled like the carcass that year, rotting in the earth behind them.

Where fibers of being once kept the two strung together; where words pulled limbs from sockets like butter; where friendships were born and will die. Where trust is torn in half with a temporary girl named Teresa.

The Bike Path.

His First Beer

Deja Vu that particular morning certainly was not welcome. A line of nostalgic clouds pillowed the horizon like sunrise sherbert, persuading Dom to smile, just like it did last time. It had the same soft glaze - all quiet and alive at the same time. If you closed your eyes, you could feel the Earth moving on it's axis.

Only thing was, back then it was Kelly laying on his stomach - not his wife, Priya. And dawn meant being awake for 15 hours - not waking up a little earlier than usual.

Yes, life was simpler. Colors had meaning. Clouds still came in shapes and weren't yet rendered or networked. And usually, they were only hunted when there weren't any waves.

"What's wrong, sweetie?" asked Priya, palming her groggy eyes. "What're you smirking at?"

"Nothing - just thinking."

"About what?"

He chuckled. "Just the sunrise. Reminded me of a something back in high school."

"Anything important?"

"Nah, just my idiot brother."

Priya shrugged and let her eyes doze off.

Close one, he thought, letting his go too.

15 years ago, Dom was here on this same beach, probably next to the same jetty, drinking his first beer as a legal adult (though not of legal drinking age). Kelly was between her freshman and sophomore year of college already and drove all the way from her UConn apartment to visit. She brought the beer.

It was a familiar dampness that brought him back. Sensory recall. He could taste the bitterness on his young tastebuds too.

Kelly stood there, toes in the water, soaking in fragmented moment. Dom couldn't remember another time before that, seeing her or any other woman besides his mother so confident in the universe, quietly taking it all in. She was beautiful, seemingly wiser with each passing day. Much more so from the last time they saw each other. He was still an amatuer to this "life" thing, only knowing life as a mere high school student.

Maybe that's what college does to you, he thought. *Maybe it hardens you to shell reality like an adult.*

Now he knows that's only experiential wisdom.

He doesn't get to drink morning beers anymore, either. *But that's a price to pay for confidence and personal growth.* He learned that from her in time. It's what helped him snag a keeper like Priya.

"I don't know how you guys do it down here! Let someone pump your gas for you. It's so weird!" Kelly laughed, turning away from the ocean and back towards him. "I got yelled at for touching the nozzle!"

"Yeah, you're supposed to stay with your car. But no one ever does that."

"It's a different world here in Jersey." She shot him a look.

Dom laughed, "You act like you've been gone for decades!"

"I mean I *was*," she nudged his elbow. "But we moved before high school. I'm a Boston girl now." She laughed.

"Yea and I bet you're a Tom Brady fan too."

"He's sooo dreamy."

They went back to the dry sand and watched the sunrise for a few more moments. Dom sipped his beer, consumed by the past, understandably so. Kelly could tell. He hadn't yet learned how to manage such intense emotions. But he was trying.

His father only died three years ago so she had to give it to him.

"Thanks for coming," Dom said. "Everyone else forgot."

Kelly sat up from his chest, smiling. "Of course *Dominic*!"

"You know I love you, right?"

"Yeah, yeah - I love you too, kid."

"If Big Carl had to choose anyone to have a first beer with me, he would've definitely picked you."

"He did always have good taste," she said. "I miss him too."

Kelly hugged him and he noted the waft of salty hair. That particular smell stuck with the patterned clouds. Deja Vu knew how to rip into your guts when it wanted to.

Back in adult life, he rubbed his nose and smiled at the horizon as Priya fell asleep on his chest again. Time danced along his neurons - familiar and yet completely different. He made mental note to call Kelly and wish her happy birthday. It was coming up next month.

What It Really Is

It's easy to forget about the noise of the world when you've got your toes on the nose. Kunu knew this well. He knew you could sense everything, hanging over the edge like Poseidon. The waves would pull you ashore, connecting you to the unfathomable powers of nature, and the only thing that made any sense was how the splash hit your ankles off the backside rail. Mortgage rates and political corruption curled away with whitewash. Heartaches melted in foam. When life shook you up, surfing kept you viable. It was his one true escape.

Kunu learned at a young age, as his father taught him, religiously paddling out every Saturday morning with a big smile on his face. Even after the family moved from Hawaii back to Jersey. It was humanizing, being out on the ocean. Papa Joe wanted to retire where he was born, but the life-lessons remained persistent. And the only thing that ever kept them out of the water were flat conditions, sometimes scattered. *Just the kind he grew up with*. The kind that drove Papa Joe to Hawaii to start a family and shape surfboards for a living.

Back when Kunu was young, Papa Joe taught him how to reach the nose of The Boat on even the flattest of days. He'd have him watch from the everyday noserider, just floating there behind the swell, studying the crossover footwork. He was a large man, but had the finesse of an MMA fighter.

"You have to feel the board," he'd say. "Stay humble and accept what you cannot change."

Kunu, still a boy, of course had little understanding of what this meant. Though he'd learn in time.

"The balance comes from your core. Keep your legs planted in the sea."

"Yes, Papa."

The Boat, of course, came with them from the islands, as it was one of the first boards Papa Joe had shaped for the Pacific Ocean. It was a big noserider longboard, painted in a forest green - the kind of modest, old school board you don't see too much on the Jersey coastlines.

Quite obviously, when asked to name it, the young Kunu shouted "Boat" because of how big it was. Standing at 8'10, it was a monster compared to the little one.

"Great name, son," he laughed.

Papa Joe had originally shaped it to surf it with his old dog, Jet (R.I.P.) back at the North Shore on the calm days. Over time, it became the bond between him and Kunu. Every Saturday morning. To this day. Even up in Jersey. If the waves were trash, they'd use it as a bench to watch the sunrise on.

Some things never change.

Other things do, though. Papa Joe was diagnosed with late stage lung cancer right after Kunu got married. "Probably from all of the fiberglass," said the Doctor, seemingly judgemental. "There aren't many options at this point."

When he passed, he left the board to Kunu. His last words, in fact. "Your children will love it," he said. "Remember what it really is."

But Kunu wouldn't go near it.

For the longest time, life went on, as it always does. He and his wife bought a home in Ocean City, New Jersey. They had three kids: a boy and two girls. Their dog grew up equally as fast. And the board sat in the garage for six years, reminding him of what it really was. It hung on the back wall so he could see it every time he got in or out of the car. Every Saturday morning, Kunu would nod as if to say, "I miss you dad," before heading to karate lessons or soccer practice.

He'd surf when he had the chance, though he'd mostly stick to the 6'1 shorty or 7' fun-shape. They were easier to transport and held lighter memories. The Boat became dusty and eventually gray.

Then, one day, Kunu had an epiphany.

It was a warm Thursday in February. Valentine's Day was around the corner and the newly appointed president had announced a ban on Muslims in the country. Kunu felt resonance of Nazi Germany through the radio during his homeward commute. He thought about his kids and their young lives. And in whatever strange direction the universe unfolds, his father's words echoed between his ears: "Remember what it really is."

"Sure thing, dad," he muttered to the dashboard.

While the world seemed to push away, he knew The Boat was the only thing that would make him feel human again. It was a no-brainer. Papa Joe would've done the same.

The routine after work was quick: unpack, surf check, wetsuit, paddle out. Luckily the waves weren't too big, otherwise he'd have to settle for the 6'1. And no way that would've worked. Only the big gun could ease his nerves.

The lineup was small - three others on their longboards, too. Eric, Bobby, and Paul, all bundled up in winter hoods and booties.

"Uh oh," Eric said. "The Boat! Haven't seen that guy in years. What's wrong?"

Kunu smiled, hiding everything as per usual. "Nah, nothing."

"Yeah, *okay!*" said Paul. "Life sucks - we get it." He paddled real quick into the next swell and rode in.

"Everything okay?" asked Eric.

"Yeah man - you good?" chimed Bobby.

"I'm good guys - thanks. Just a rough day."

"I heard. Can you believe this orange douchebag?"

Kunu looked down and cupped the water.

Eric blurted, "Sindhu said her family is going back to India. They don't want to support this asshole anymore."

"I can't blame them," said Bobby.

"That sucks, man, I'm sorry," said Kunu. "Is she going with them? What're you guys going to do?"

"She doesn't know yet. *I* don't even know yet."

"I'm sorry bud," said Bobby. "I hope it works out."

Eric sighed. "Thanks guys." A wave strolled through, "This is you," he said to Kunu.

Kunu paddled and fell into the wave with a familiar ease. The Boat was always good for that.

With his feet planted in the sea, Kunu felt himself let go as he tiptoed his way to the nose of the board and back again. His shoulders loosened up and the air on his face felt like fire. While the world fell silent, the genes of his father's heart bubbled up over the rails and helped him crossover with a certain finesse as if he'd never forget what it really was.

How to Live Your Life to the Fullest

It goes like this:

Step 1:
Eat entire Johnny Macs' bar pie at happy hour.

Step 2:
Cap out at 3 beers because you have to drive home.

Step 3:
Receive text from cousin that Grandpa is in the ICU again.

Step 4:
Stop home to change out of work clothes, brush your teeth, drink some water and some coffee.

Step 5:
Drive to Jersey Shore Medical.

Step 6:
Find Grandpa is okay - stabilized in room 34C, barely conscious, pumped full of drugs.

Step 7:
Call mom and dad to let them know. Leave a voicemail that you don't mean to ruin their vacation but Grandpa is in the hospital and to call when they get this.

Step 8:
Stay the night, slouched over and alone in a really uncomfortable chair because no one in this goddamn family cares.

Step 9:
Have a heartattack when Grandpa wakes in the middle of the night, gasping for air like a fish out of water. Call the nurse. She'll give him more drugs. She'll also have an attitude about it.

Step 10:
Tread sleep lightly for the remaining few hours until dawn, finding solace in the never-ending commotion of hospital life.

Step 11:
Go home to rest when Aunt Carly and Uncle Tom show up, pretending to care long enough for the will to be made out. Smile and nod, even though you know what they're really here for.

Step 12:
Drive home slowly, hugging the shoulder lane on your tippy toes like mom's waist.

Step 13:
Become startled when a bird fatally strikes the window and flops over dead in your rearview, playing the divebomb game that all birds seem to play with traffic.

<u>Step 14</u>:
Get home and immediately collapse on the sofa. It doesn't matter if you keep your shoes on.

<u>Step 15</u>:
Wake up after the sun is already down, find several texts from Uncle Tom that say they've decided to put Gramps out of his misery, and that it's what he would've wanted anyway, and to please call your parents to let them know. It will piss you off because he's an inlaw and it's not even his father yet he still calls him 'Gramps' like you think it's okay or something.

<u>Step 16</u>:
Think about the time that Grandpa gave you ice cream for breakfast while you were 8 and your parents were on vacation. Remember his words: "Life is short, enjoy it while you can."

<u>Step 17</u>:
Find the hole in your apartment that overlooks the ocean; the one where you think about dying. Open the window and breathe in some salt air. It'll relax your lungs.

<u>Step 18</u>:
Contemplate leaving this shithole state. Think about what it would take to cut ties from the toxic people in your life but ultimately realize that it isn't a good idea and you don't really have the money anyway.

<u>Step 19</u>:

Watch the seagulls and herrings ride breeze patterns with a carelessness that you wish you could posses. Think about the bird that hit your car.

Step 20:
Try to understand that the universe has a plan and that it will all be okay.

Step 21:
Realize it will all be okay. Be mindful of your life and your small slice of universe by the sea.

Step 22:
Dig out your black tie, your black jacket. Dust off your dress shoes.

Step 23:
Realize your time and fortune in waking up everyday. Decide to make an extra effort every day; to grow wiser and more accepting of the cards you're dealt. See loved ones more often.

Step 24:
Breathe in. Breathe out. Repeat.

Seasick

"I'm tired, aren't you tired?" I ask my father, on bikes riding up to the beach.

"Not really," he shrugs. "But then again, I'm always tired."

There are things I want to tell him. Emotions I want to express. He can tell when I have something to say.

"What's on your mind?" he asks.

I've been treading water for a while, seasick in the riptide of space and time just offshore. Kicking my feet around seems easy compared to everything else.

It's hard for me to admit that I'm depressed with the progressive back and forth destruction of our planetary existence. Of our political leaders and humanitarians and their disregard for things beyond money and the elite.

Holding this in would cut future holes in my chest. It's not easily accepted by people my age or even those older. They choke up. They get anxious. They are set in their grooves already. And younger individuals haven't yet been exposed to the perspective. At least consciously.

People don't like things that change their understanding truth.

But it sloshes around my stomach anyway, pixels

painted to my eyelids like beads of nostalgic decay; salty infirmities line my cognizance like a string of lights around receding hairlines. We were programmed from birth with no say in the matter; beliefs already imprinted on our neocortex.

One day you wake up and realize you've wasted a chunk of your life, pulling the limbs from sockets of spiders and centipedes, then the next you're paying bills for things you don't need and concepts you don't believe in. The tide rises and falls, waves settle along the shoreline, and the neon shells stuck between your toes glue together any remaining shreds of eternal organicness that you might have left.

You become seasick. You don't know how to fix it. You feel incorrigible and remain silent in fear of the adhesive label that'll get pasted to your forehead.

I don't say any of this. Instead, I say, "Nah, nothing."

"Just say it. The freedom of speech is a luxury that not everyone has."

"No, dad, I'd rather not risk being labeled a conspiracy whackjob by those who don't understand things deeper than their current understanding."

"Okay, son."

An evolution of flip flops and salty skin, sun-bleached hair follicles painted in the soft, southeast breeze has given me an opportunistic reality of all things not real. The numbness of humanity, sheep in the herd, ready to give up any intellectual progress for a millisecond of material wealth. The kind of numbness that will rot with the earth like the flesh stretched across my muscles. Not the styrofoam littered in the shorebreak, or the spiritual people who've yet to see the stones they've engraved at the pits of their eyes. No. I refuse. I'm not a complex algorithm of controlled hierarchy. I am human. I am organic. My bones are recycled stardust. My shell is temporary. The chains that bound them are invisible. *There's a difference.* Can't everyone else see that?

I look around aimlessly. "Some people just don't get it," I say.

Everyone is looped in parking garages of sand and concrete, trapped by their own bleeding hope and stubborn blindness to the elitist systems designed to destroy the world in their never-ending quench for corporative power.

"They're caught up in things that don't matter."

He keeps peddling, looking ahead at the traffic. Still focused on the task at hand.

"Dad, I'm not crazy. Am I?"

"Of course not, son. You are exactly what you need to be." He smiles. "We're all tired sometimes."

We get to the beach and stretch for the afternoon workout. He dives right in, heading out towards the first marker.

And there I was. At the water. Ready to leave this

sunken planet. Ready to colonize another solar system by myself if I had to. My father has already started his second lap around the buoy. I couldn't focus and felt it in the pit of my stomach. I never knew what to say or do or think so I end up doing the only thing that's ever made sense and plant myself in the cold sand near the waterline, listening to the waves lap at my toes, holding in nausea while contemplating some way to escape the Orwellian trap that has somehow become so real in this time period of human existence.

When he comes back around for his third lap, I finally wake up with a deep breath.

"Fuck it," I mutter, and dive into the shorebreak. As I float weightless back to the surface, I feel like someone new and start swimming towards the buoy.

In the Backyard (pt. 3)

Some stale, leftover sunset gives the distant trees a golden definition. The bottom trunks are dark and hold creatures, preparing for the incoming storm, listening to the roots lick their lips. Ash and soot, steady as they are, roll across the sky like waves, slowly absorbing sunlight slices on the painted treetops. The breeze talks to me, to my dog and my house, to my soul while we sit in the backyard with resilience.

"Will you be okay?" I ask them.

"We will be fine," the mighty oak says, shaking the leafy air out of his branches. "You should consider shelter. This is a big one."

I nod. My dog looks over, ears perched, thinking he heard what was (most likely) in my head.

An influent breeze streams the hair on my arm. Beads of pressure tighten inside my lungs, the system moving at it's own pace, humidity seeping into my pores. All of the trees air out their leaves simultaneously. The dune grass dances in echoes of Friday night's parties; fluttering in the rhythm of universe like everything is okay.

"Talk to me," says the one coated in ivy, "You seem distraught."

"Over nothing," I say. "Nothing.'

"Then you slouch in grey for nothing?"

I smile at where the face would be. "And for everything."

The wind ruffles my ears. All of the trees laugh. My irides soak in iridescence, pasting colors on my spine with a gluestick and patience. I am nothing and I am everything. In the backyard.

When The World Ends...

1.

That year was a tough one for everyone, let alone James. Instagram was bought out by Facebook for a billion dollars. Hurricane Sandy punched local summer in the face during October. And the world was supposed to end according to the Aztec calendar. (It didn't.) It was also a leap year.

However, James Haddon was too busy experiencing the human condition to care about those things. Early on in his 20's, trying to make sense of the world, he'd already become a cog in the system; yet to discover the universe.

He spent his days stocking shelves at a liquor store; his nights dedicated to the last two classes of his soon-to-be-worthless, over-priced Bachelor's Degree from Monmouth University. The planet seemed to grow larger every day.

"What do you wanna do tonight?" asked Brynn from her beach towel, tanning the backside of her legs.

"Uhm," grunted James, "dunno - what were you thinking?"

"I think Jamie said they were gonna pre-game at the backhouse. Wanna start there and see where it goes?"

"Sure."

"What's wrong?" she blurted.

James adjusted himself in his chair, leaning it back closer to the sand, pulling his sunglasses back over his receding hairline. "Nothing," he sighed.

"Well you seem pissed off."

"Okay."

"Why are you pissed off?"

"I'm not." He really wasn't. Just tired of always being accused of it.

"Then why are you making that face?"

"What face?"

She scrunched her nose and brow together. James felt like she was mocking him. She wasn't. "Like this," she laughed.

2.
At work, a box of wine split open as James picked it up from the stack. He grumbled and cleaned it up, cursing the world. It was Friday; the thought of meeting Brynn at the beach after his unusual morning shift was the only thing that kept him

going. That night you were supposed to be able to see Venus for the last time in this century.

3.

Tonight was the night. James had been contemplating this for weeks. His buddy, Will, just broke up with his college girlfriend because she started dropping blatant hints towards diamond rings. Beyonce's "Single Ladies" was still a relatively popular bar song at the time.

"I don't know what to do."

Will bunny-hopped his cruiser up the curb. "It sounds like you do though."

"I guess." James sat back on his, feeling lost in a sea of asphalt.

"Look man. If you're not happy, you're not happy. It's no one's fault. But you have to talk this out, regardless."

"Yeah."

"And if you guys lost that sexy spark like you were saying… then your instincts are probably right."

They pulled up to Happy Hour, Thursday night. James was skipping Astronomy; a freshman level science elective he'd intentionally saved for his last semester.

"That's why I broke up with Rebecca." Will locked his bike to the stop sign and shrugged. "We were on different pages. We talked it out and felt it wasn't worth wasting each other's time."

4.

It was raining. James spent the day searching for the sun in a sky of grey. Then again at night, when the moon never came. Particles of universe kept life balanced. Will's brother, Paul, was skateboarding around shirtless. Up the driveway, down the driveway, up the driveway, and down again. Repeat a couple hundred times.

"Dude - that's F'd up."

"Yeah."

"I mean even after she said all that bullshit two weeks ago?"

"Yep! I told her I bought a ring too!" James laughed, attributing his loudness to one or more of the various chemicals soaking his bloodstream.

"Wait what?! You didn't, did you?"

"No, of course not."

"That's cold!" Will laughed.

"I know!"

For some reason those particular tears reminded James of the ones from when Michael Jackson died a few years back. Or when Obama was elected and they stormed the campus greens with the other drunk kids, banging buckets and pans, blaring that "A Milli" rap remix by APT, "Obama, Obama" from speakers in the windows.

But also like the ones from Julie's wedding back in February. Brynn was a crier. He knew it'd cut her deeply - one of those lifelong scars that would one day haunt her future husband.

"I knew it'd make her feel worse," he said, shaking his head. "Faked it the whole fuckin' time."

"Well she deserved it after this bullshit."

"Yeah," said James. "Where'd you get these by the way? I think Paul's really kicked in..."

5.
"I got this round," said Will.

"Dude, no. Come on, that's three in a row. My turn."

"Nope. No way. You got a rough night ahead of you. Let me be a good friend. It's the least I could do."

"Fine." James swigged the last of his pint glass and placed it on the counter. He knew Will was only trying to get enough beers into him so he wouldn't back out last minute. "But I'm not your wingman."

At the bar Will tried picking up the older women sitting next to them, bringing up the London Olympics and Michael Phelps. Like he even cared about having a wingman in the first place. Columns got crowded quickly, so when nothing panned out they finished one final round and went to Bar-A to set things in motion with Brynn.

On the ride over, James thought about how he'd phrase it:
> "I don't think this is working out."
> "I think it's best we cut ties."
> "I don't love you anymore."
None of them sounded right. He'd figure it out.

6.
"Wait she broke up with you?" asked Tom, sipping his beer.

"Yeah." The world felt heavy on his shoulders. His pint glass tasted like ash.

"But didn't you..." he trailed off.

"Yep. Two weeks ago. And she convinced me to give us a second chance."

"... just so she wouldn't have to cancel the party?"

James nodded. Swigged his beer, seemingly aimless.

"I mean it **WAS** a surprise party," chimed in Zach. "There was a live band and everything."

Everyone shot him a look. He grinned.

"Hey man I know it sucks," said Tom. "But this is what you wanted, remember?"

"Yeah."

"Plus," said Zach, "you can spend the ring money on something for yourself! Didn't you want to buy a new car?"

"I'm going to look at Jeeps next weekend."

"Nice! The 2013's are probably on the lot already!"

"Yeah."

7.

Mid August. Early dinner at Kaya's Kitchen on Main Street. James had the bean burger and Brynn the kale.

"I think you were right," she said.

At first, he wasn't sure what she was talking about. Then the bell went off.

"We aren't working."

"What do you mean?" His organs dropped.

"I think we should break up."

James sunk into the booth, into the concrete and then the earth. He didn't know how to respond.

"We aren't on the same page anymore. You're always off doing your own thing. We haven't slept together in weeks."

"But just the other day... when I suggested this... you said no. You convinced me that we were just in a rough patch. Just to keep trying."

"Well yeah. But I changed my mind."

"What do you mean you changed your mind? You threw me a surprise birthday party. How do you just 'change your mind' after doing something like that? All of our friends and family were there."

"So what if they were?! I can't help how I feel."

"No. You mean you didn't want embarrass yourself by cancelling the party and telling everyone why."

"Look I don't see what the big deal is. This is what you wanted."

James stared at the last bite of his fake burger. "I bought a ring after that you know. What you did, with that party, inviting everyone we know. It changed me. Made me realize. It's being set as we speak."

"I'm sorry," shrugged Brynn.

"Yeah," said James.

8.

"Wait this isn't the way to Jamie's house."

Brynn gripped the steering wheel, trying to hold back a smile. "I know, I just gotta stop home first."

They turned into her parents' driveway, completely devoid of cars. Unusual for the Belmar beach house. "Where is everyone?" asked James, pulling himself from the car.

Brynn could not hold it back any longer. The nerves fell right off her face, all her teeth shining in the setting sun like tic-tacs. "I dunno," she said, chewing on bluff.

He turned the corner, around into the back, and was bombarded by a crowd screaming "SURPRISE!" at the top of their lungs. The faces were immediately familiar: his family, his friends, long lost mentors and coaches. Even some of their friends from school.

The band in the garage doorway yelled "Happy Birthday James!" and started playing a cover Fun's "We are Young" with a mellow radiance.

Something beamed inside of him that he hadn't felt in a long time. A little wedge of life reminding him of his human. That one little micro-pixel of time. James felt the light switch click over in his heart. He realized how lucky he was to have someone like Brynn to help keep his head on straight, to keep his universe sewn together with soul. Between all the hugs and high fives, he made up his mind. He was going to buy a ring.

9.

Will and James went inside and found Brynn and her friends. Several drinks later, when the girls stepped aside for a restroom break, Will leaned over and said, "So? Did you set it up yet?"

"Not yet," replied James. "What are you going to do when we leave?"

"I'm going to hit on her friends. What did you think I was going to do?"

"How is that any different than what you're doing now?"

James slugged his beer and went to go get another round for the table. When he came back, the girls were laughing at Will, who turned and winked at James upon his return.

"So, Brynn," said Will, "James tells me that your friends aren't very good at taking shots."

There was an uproar towards James, who shook his head at Will. "What? It's true. Sam can't handle anything without juice in it."

"Heyyyy," smiled Sam. "That's not nice! Screw you! If you're buying, line up the tequila!"

"Oh don't say that! You're gonna give this guy the wrong idea." Brynn pointed at Will.

"You're on!" Will shot up and went directly to the bar.

James turned to Brynn, ready to spit fire, trigger like a hairpin. "Hey I gotta talk to you about something tomorrow after work. When we're not drunk." He laughed. "Meet at the beach at 4? Normal spot?"

Brynn glanced around at her silent friends and sipped her beer. "Okay," she said, hesitantly. "Am I in trouble?"

Her friends laughed. James did not. Will came back with 6 shots of Patron. "Goodnight ladies," he said, slinging one of them back.

10.

"I thought you were going to do it last night," said Will over coffee and dark sunglasses.

"Me too, but I wussed out." James shook his head. "I want to do it when we're not drunk."

"There's your first mistake."

"How do you figure?"

"A drunken break-up is beautiful! In no other period of our lives will it ever be socially acceptable to express the very idea of drunken decision-making, and yet still enjoy watching as everything burns to the ground in a matter of minutes."

"That sounds horrible."

"Better than drawing it out for two years."

"Yeah I guess." James sipped his coffee, waiting outside on the patio of Belmar Bagel for his turn to do what cogs do.

"So today? After your shift?"

"After my shift."

11.

James drove straight to the beach after work. He was sweaty. Tired. And completely empty inside. Radical Something's "Valentine" spilled out his car's windows. Summer was only half over. The shell of his being rattled around like leftover pretzels at the bottom of a bag. He was ready. August would be better.

"Hey I'm here," he said, turning off the engine. "Where are you?"

"Up on 12th Ave. Just before the drainage."

"See you in a minute." He tucked his phone back into his pocket and took a deep breath.

Brynn sat softly in the sand, eyes as straight as the horizon. The air between them was thick. James had trouble breathing in the residual humidity, even though the sun was behind them, his childhood breathing patterns never left. The sunset was wearing warm colors, like makeup. It was supposed to be a fresh start.

"So that's it then?"

Seagulls cawed at each other just down the crest of tide. Children laughed in the lowtide shorebreak.

"After 4 years we're done? Just like that?"

"I guess so," said James, tonguing the gums of his teeth.

"What happened to 'I'll love you forever' and 'You're my soulmate'?"

"I dunno, people change."

She didn't like that answer so she pulled her sunglasses down over her eyes. James knew there were tears behind them. She didn't think he did.

"Look this isn't your fault," he said. "It's me."

No response. He looked around, trying to see the powdered clouds and sheers of light, but summertime sadness held him by the throat. "We can still be friends," he said.

"No we can't." She looked at him with that same sour face. "I have to go," she said, and then left.

James sat in the sand, watching the sky fade from blue to yellow to orange to pink to purple to black. The tide crept out away from him until he could see the far side of jetty. The evening haze wore off and he went home, alongside the crowds going back out. A *21 Jump Street* reboot came out later that night.

12.

James was in Will's basement when she texted him.

"Can we talk?" It said. "I need to get some things off my chest."

He replied; "Sure - let's meet at Stay Gold Cafe? 10 mins?" It felt wrong sending the message. But everyone always told him he was too nice.

After he sent it, he looked up at Will who was already glaring at him.

"Dude," he said. "Don't do it."

"I have to. I'm not like that, man."

"You're gonna regret it." Will fiercely sipped his beer. "You always do."

13.

James arrived first and ordered an overpriced iced coffee. He knew Will was right - it occurred to him when the cashier gave him singles back for change from a $20. In a few months, he'd have to somehow pay for Obamacare.

"Sorry, I'm late," said Brynn, climbing up the barstool. "Hit traffic..."

"No worries, what's up?"

"I don't think we should do this. I think we should give it another shot."

James felt limp, like the plane banners flapping at the beach. "Why? Don't you feel like we were forcing it?"

"Yeah, I guess. But that was my fault. I stopped trying. I fell into a funk after last semester. You know how that feels. Right?"

The barista walked up and asked Brynn if she wanted anything. She said no.

"I just don't feel right without you." She turned back to him.

James sipped the watery coffee, contemplating his life in the future. There had always been a warm body next to him. Much like the job, the house, the kids. Though, he could never quite make out the face on that body. Maybe it was her. Maybe she'd taken off the mask and wanted to help pull him from the machine.

"Yeah, okay," he said, the tide rising in his heart. "Why not?"

Sleepy Eyes

I had those sleepy eyes. The kind like a slow pulsating trap door, leaking light between cracks of reality. It was the start of August and our bikes appreciated any down time they could get. Not too humid. Not too hot. A Tuesday under the best kind of summer sun.

I was always down to watch stars pierce the sky and then melt with our closest one. So was Katherine. We were moceanless and fully prepared to sleep on the beach through morning if we wanted. Our chairs had been properly rotated; stationed perfectly in direct sunlight, yet close enough to smell the breeze rolling off the waves.

"Let's try to beat out the bennys," I said.

Katherine nodded, probably already well ahead of me. I dug into our bag and pulled out my book. "I love where we live," she mumbled.

"Me too."

Every afternoon our hearts swelled in size. I'd grown to love when it kicked me in the soul.

The out-of-towners, the kind with table umbrellas and camping chairs and wheely coolers, they usually stayed until sunset and then left. I imagine they felt the need to get their money's worth for the badge. Or maybe they felt the calling too. Whatever it was, they'd eventually notice their crispy shoulders and call it quits.

They made for some of the best people-watching.

"We got this," I smile. "The lifeguards leave in 10 minutes. Belmar keeps them til 6 now."

Sometimes, we'd stay just to get a head start on the next morning and claim a good spot near the water. Other times we only wanted to see the sunrise.

"They don't stand a chance," Katherine smiled. She sat up and prowled around in a glance. "I can see Lobster Larry over there already starting to pack up his kids."

"They're done for!"

I don't know why I even bothered trying to read. The second my eyes fell back into the book, I dozed off. Vonnegut was not enough to keep me focused.

So it goes.

I dreamt of pork roll egg and cheese sandwiches and Turnstile iced coffee. Every so often, the southeast wind would kiss the flesh of my face to keep me grounded in our formidable reality. Even in my REM sleep.

When I came to, we were alone. "Hey babe, what time is it?" I looked around, the sun cresting behind Ocean Ave, a soft chill floating in from the Southeast. We were the only ones on the sand for five blocks in either direction. Katherine had a towel wrapped around her shoulders, snugged up on her beach chair, still wearing her woven sunhat from the 90's. My book lay flat in the sand, dog-eared on the same page I'd opened it on.

"Babe?"

No response.

I went down to the water and gazed into the flat endlessness. It called for me, as she always does. My lungs were balloons, inflated with salty air, accepting myself and my present moment for everything that it was. Stars pinned holes in the horizon. I felt their light pressed up against my bare chest, chewing on my existence. They served as reminders: we were still here and fate had dealt us a pretty fortunate hand.

I couldn't help but smile.

Then, as if it wasn't even my decision, I jumped right into the shorebreak one last time before dark. My eyes were sleepy and the mid-tide waves were just right.

Surf Check

A southeast breeze painted our energy with afternoon frequencies, me and my dog. We were creatures of sand and salt water. Lost in our own hearts. Vibrations awry. By then, our summer feet were on point, finally adjusted to the excessive heat around us. We were just two simple beings, sentient enough to catch eager ripples in our lungs. Regardless of the humidity.

Doyle stretched his legs, grinning at me with fangs like a true predator. I smiled back. He shook his coat and trotted up along me, taking after my stride. Our anxieties leaked out between our teeth.

"This way," I muttered, pulling him around the corner, up to the edge of the inlet jetty. "Another week and you'll be able to see the waves up close again."

"Sir, you can't have your dog up here," said one of the patrol officers leaning on the gazebo. "There's a dog beach around the corner, off Riverside."

"I know, I apologize," I cut him off. "Just wanted to check the surf."

"Well be quick," grunted the other one, adjusting his aviator sunglasses.

We were hybrids; only operating at 100% capacity between May and September. The rest of the year we waited for summer. Even these khaki'd beach cops.

"2 minutes," the first one spat.

Doyle gruffed, compelling me to shush him (against my will). He knew just as well as I did that there was a dog beach out on Fisherman's Cove. But that would defeat the purpose of checking the surf. Inside the canal where there weren't any waves. Unless there was a hurricane.

Plus, the breeze was heavier at the edge of the beachwalk. It painted lines on our hearts.

"Okay, thanks." I forced a smile.

The swell grew from last week and the forecast called for some decent surf later that evening. Hurricane season approached quickly that year too. After Sandy hit us, I thought I'd never go back in the water. I know Doyle was nervous to even go outside. But something about the sand and the salt kept calling to us. We got over it quicker than all my ex-girlfriends.

"Alright bud, let's head back," I said to Doyle. "Thank you, officers."

They nodded and went back to pretending to be awake.

Doyle and I went off, eagerly waiting for the lifeguards to get off duty. Something in the air kept our lungs inflated and we slipped into another August evening, dripping in sweat and positive energy from a simple stroll up to the beach. Somehow, the ocean does right. Every single time.

Seaside in August

Monday. Melted ice cream,
dripping through the cracks of boardwalk.

A papermoon pasted on dusk.

Air wisps cool off the ocean,
humidity dusting the horizon in makeup.

Swells dull, gently swaying the inlet buoys.

Herrings squalling over schools of fish,
picked clean in the breeze.

Gulls sweeping through piles of washed-up
mollusks.

Sheers of sunset, cut apart
by razored clouds and prisms of light.

Toes disappearing, calm sand near the sea.

The lapping tide,
humming in harmony with all the sad hearts of
August.

Still

I found you outside of Parkerhouse, a summertime sadness soaking your bones while August faded into September around us. Kids reluctantly dragged from the beach to go back-to-school shopping, tans worn pale as Earth's equilibrium leveled out to more depressing temperatures. Sure - local summer was ahead of us, bottled-up in our chests like sea glass. It churned our edges dull with a mindset back to reality. Forget the boys you kissed, the nights you spent sleeping on the sand under stars and lifeguard stands. Beach combers might've replaced the alarm on your phone, but not the ones in your heart. Forget about June's beautiful weather and July's endless potential. Forget the road trips, the weddings, the camping, and backhouse lovers. All of those things were great - but they're behind you, scraping calcium from the pit of your spine. They are pleasant memories distracting you from what is squared right in front of you. The present. The future. The rest of your life. Reminiscing about those days is good in small doses, preferably with other people. But like any other drug, nostalgia will fog your focus in negative haze. Your neocortex is a dangerous tool. You must remember to look forward. Wake up with tomorrow's sunrise, even if it doesn't come until 7, with scattered snow showers and freezing temperatures. No - celebrate that change. It is proof that you are alive. That you're still breathing. That the sadness of August is merely infrastructure of your personal growth. Every year. Every time. It shows the patterns of which you paint with consciousness. I realize that might not be the first thing you think of when you spill onto the street in Sea Girt after dark. But if you give yourself a chance to understand, to see the light of the universe instead of the backlit screen on your phone. The happiness will find you on it's own. And if you spread that love honestly, it will come back around next summer. Trust me.

Reflections of Summer

When the sun crowns the treetops and buildings behind us, we move from the porch to the patio. Salty hair and beery lips, laughing, stacking wood for a fire. Smiles soaked in sunshine and tanlines. It was time.

A few blocks down, Bar A throws a siren to kickoff local summer, echoing between my fence like a distant buoy. Red Hot Chili Peppers. Sublime. At one point, Lil John screaming "SHOTS!" Some songs just last forever.

Someone passes out refills from stowed coolers between our beach chairs. The fire spits smoke into the New Jersey atmosphere. A few houses over, someone has the same idea. We can hear their laughs between breaks in music.

"Are you guys ready to go back?" Nick inquires. "When does school start?"

Allison laughs and swigs her wine, tired of answering the same question all week. "Tuesday, she says. "But my classroom's all ready."

"Yeah," I say. "Though I'm never ready for summer to end."

We clink beer cans and he goes back to SnapChatting pictures of Bobby, who's fallen asleep in his chair, bronze and cherried from being on the beach all day. The dogs run around the yard, chasing each other in content. Dune grass wafts in the breeze like seaweed.

Our fates aligning like hummingbirds, an ocean of matter floating around us. Allison and Anna make plans for an upcoming Friday night dinner party while Carl and I sketch ideas for a screenplay. The world is around us. The air, a soft northeast wind, brings soundwaves and low tide to our ears and noses. Reflections of summer, reinforcing just how lucky we are to be alive in this moment, living at the edge of the country, forever a beach kid in all of us.

Between the Sun and Some Shade

I was sitting in the backyard trying to make sense of it all when she brought me a beer. We cheersed and kissed and she went back inside to leave me with my thoughts. Life in New Jersey.

"Thank you!" I yelled as she stepped inside.

"You're welcome," she echoed back through the open windows.

It was September, the leaves still green. My heart patterned properly for local summer. I had time vacillated between light particles.

First I sat in the sun, and then I sat in some shade. I stared at the jet stream clouds and listened to the world, etching things into my neocortex. The sun and moon, a memory of stars opaque with blue, soaking through my heart like white blood cells. I inhaled an afternoon and exhaled what we've all been looking for. The universe was still.

"Do you want a book or something?" Her voice leaked out the screen door, which we could finally open again.

"I'm good, babe, thanks!"

In the distance, through the trees and dried up grass, the sun set in hues of orange and red and pink like a small firepit. My lungs sipped at some residual humidity and I smiled. She'd probably never understand my meditative serenity. Few might. But she'd never judge me for that. She'd never take it from me. She understood my understanding.

When the clouds went purple, it finally hit me. Something inside of me knew. The purpose of it all.

Centered on my radar, a small blip of New Jersey, right in the stillness of crazy. Exactly me, whatever I am, a meatbag skeleton composed of recycled stardust, the reason for all being, my existence on this planet, in this universe. A coincidence of space and time. A circle.

I found it.

The laughter of children and barking dogs brought me there; a time and space made just for me, where no other will experience just exactly what I do. I was here for whatever reason fate has had and that was my tranquility. (Not that'd I'd ever be able to explain it.)

I can only hope you'll one day find it too.

Seas the Day

I locked our bikes up against the boardwalk railing outside of Eastern Lines. It was a Saturday and the smell of pork roll wafted south with the wind rolling off the jetty. It led us blindly, splashing into the sand and trekking through sponsor tents and art galleries setting up their merch. We aimed for 17th ave with smiles laced across our sleeves.

"I think I see them," said Katherine. "That's Marc's hair. Definitely."

Katherine set her alarm early so we could get some Turnstile Coffee and post up a good spot near the guard stand. Our friends beat us to the shoreline, but luckily held similar standards for their spots.

"Yep! That's his Zelda shirt."

"They got a good spot too!"

I laughed. "Holler at that cutty spot!"

"Perfect for these bagels."

The Belmar Pro had always been a staple for us; this in-between phase of local summer and early fall. Our bathing suits and our hair nagged us for those last few salty adventures before the frost settled in around Halloween.

Today was for the experts. The big shots. The guys and girls from California and Hawaii who could pump into a wave that I wouldn't be able to catch with a boogie board. But ultimately... this event was for us. For the locals. For our beloved beach chairs and leftover tans and beautiful Saturday mornings with coffee and Jameson. It was for the love of being on the beach at 8am in September without all the bennys. For the love of the day.

"Hey guys!" said Jess, standing up from her chair to hug us.

"Hiiiii," sung Katherine. "Did ya find good parking?"

"Yeah, not bad," Marc turned to me and pointed towards Dunkin Donuts. "Just left of the shop."

We high-fived cause it was Saturday and we hadn't seen each other in a few months. Marc moved to Baltimore some years ago for work. But he was still a local at heart. Still had the knack for spots.

"What heat is this?" asked Katherine.

"Not sure," replied Marc. "It's the second one we've seen but I think they've been going since 7 or 8."

"Looks like Mens' quarters."

We posted up next to them, waiting for the sun to peek through the day-old-cotton-candy clouds. Everything was right. Our hearts swelled with the tide coming in; reggae softly jamming the speakers between commentary; smiles pasted to our faces.

After a few waves, Marc turned to the three of us again - Jess included - to say "hashtag blessed" with a smile on his face. "Want to go cruise the tents?" he asked, politely waiting for us to finish eNJoying our bagels.

Katherine crumpled up her bag, having already woofed hers down. "Sure!"

We stumble behind the announcing booth, sifting through Jetty t-shirts and SurfRider stickers. Eventually, Katherine and I end up at Corey Hudson's art tent. He's a local artist who'd been collecting and transforming washed-up Sandy debris into astute crafts. One of his signs - a beat-up, polished handsaw - hung on the fence in the sun: "Seas the Day - NJ" it said.

"I like that one," she said, pointing to it.

I nod in accord. Marc and Jess trotted up after signing up for a surfboard giveaway. "That one's cool," said Jess, pointing to the sunburst shape of New Jersey, hung next to the saw. "Yeah it is," Marc agreed.

Katherine and I grinned at each other to acknowledge the dumb couple-moment we see everywhere since discovering the 7's.

"Carpe diem!" shouted Marc, stuffing his Ocean Jeep swagbag with stickers. "Let's go back and catch this heat before high tide gets here."

We strode back to our chairs, the entire Belmar shoreline alive for the day, eager to watch professional athletes do their thing. The sun eventually came through the scattered clouds, reminding me to seas the day. Everything'll be okay. Every experience in this life brings us back to the beach anyway.

Let Me Tell You A Little Something About Local Summer

There's no such thing as local summer. Never heard of it.

Quotes

Here are some quotes to ponder between now and the next book:

- "The curtain rises on a vast primitive wasteland, not unlike certain parts of New Jersey." — Woody Allen

- "I used to wonder why people made New Jersey jokes. I don't anymore." — E.J. Copperman

- "Artificial Intelligence leaves no doubt that it wants its audiences to enter a realm of pure fantasy when it identifies one of the last remaining islands of civilization as New Jersey." — Godfried Danneels

- "The aim of art is to represent not the outward appearance of things, but their inward significance." — Aristotle

- "That by dreams I have received help, as for other things, so in particular, how I might stay my casting of blood, and cure my dizziness, as that also that happened to thee in Cajeta, as unto Chryses when he prayed by the seashore." — Marcus Aurelius, from *Meditations*

- "[H]e was experiencing what the Stoics would call a sympatheia - a connectedness with the cosmos. The French philosopher Pierre Hadot has referred to it as the "oceanic feeling." A sense of belonging to something larger, of realizing that "human things are an infinitesimal point in the immensity." It is in these moments that we're not only free but drawn toward important questions: *Who am I? What am I doing? What is my role in this world?*" — Ryan Holiday, from *Ego is the Enemy*

- "Focus on the moment, not the monsters that may or may not be up ahead." — Ryan Holiday, from *The Obstacle Is the Way*

- "In the depth of winter, I finally learned that within me there lay an invincible summer." — Albert Camus

- "When we watch the waves on these summer days she makes everything alright." — Radical Something, "Tequila Kiss"

- "Those who live by the sea can hardly form a single thought of which the sea would not be part." — Hermann Broch

- "We are tied to the ocean. And when we go back to the sea, whether it is to sail or to watch - we are going back to whence we came." — John F. Kennedy

- "You are what you think." — Ray Kurzweil, *How To Create A Mind*

- "The best advice I can give is to enjoy yourself more. Not have fun more. But to **enjoy** yourself more. Fun, to me, is sort of these quick spikes of celebration and partying or whatever. But enjoying something is more sustainable. Just dial in on what will make you sustainably happy." — Dave Camarillo, from *The Tim Ferriss Show*, episode #196

- "I almost feel cheated if I don't hear the ocean. The rhythm of the ocean is just so beautiful. And so the rhythm of life. I feel so blessed to be on it and to hear it." — Shep Gordan, from *The Tim Ferriss Show*, episode #184

- "Consider the decision to write this book - I never made that decision. Rather, the idea of the book decided that for me." — Ray Kurzweil, *How To Create A Mind*

Bio

Glen Binger is just a beach kid from New Jersey. He writes books and helps people learn how to learn. His work can be found via Google, along with many other answers to the questions burning your guts.